The Classified Hustle

The Classified Hustle

A Novel by Jerome Blake

Liberated Minds, LLC
Everett, Washington

Book Production by Cypress House

Paperback ISBN: 979-8-9931009-0-6
Ebook ISBN: 979-8-9931009-1-3
Library of Congress Number 2025920801

2 4 6 8 9 7 5 3 1

First edition

Printed in the United States of America

In Loving Memory of
Michelle "Fatty" Blake
and
Kathleen "Auntie Kat" Ardson

The Origins

Aurora, Illinois, Summer 1996

"The Chicago Bulls are once again NBA champions, after defeating the Seattle Supersonics 4-2 in a best of 7 series, with a final score of 87-75!" the TV announcer proclaimed.

"I'm gonna be a NBA champion just like Michael Jordan!" yelled Charlie to his younger brother Delvon.

"Ha-ha-ha, this nigga is funny. You can't—"

Fatty interrupted Delvon, shouting over the sounds of the song *Outstanding* by The Gap Band that was playing in the dining room, where the adults were sitting around the table playing a game of spades. "You better watch your mouth, lil' boy—what I tell you bout that word?!"

Ignoring Fatty, "Oh, yeah? Set it up right now!" Charlie demanded.

Shawn, their baby brother, cut in excitedly, "I wanna play too! Let me play, let me play!"

Delvon ran out of the room and came back in with a wire coat hanger, which he began to bend and shape into a circle to form a basketball rim. "Where's the ball?" Charlie asked.

"I'm not usin my socks, we used mines last time and now I can't find 'em," Charlie said. "Well I guess we ain't playin then, 'cause I ain't usin mine neither!"

Little Shawn jumped up and down, shouting, "Let me play, let me—"

Interrupting him, Fatty yelled again, "Y'all better let my baby play or nobody gonna play a mothafuckin thang!"

Delvon lowered his voice, "How she even hear us? I thought she was playin cards?"

"Don't you worry bout what I'm doin," Fatty shouted from the table. "Y'all gonna let my baby play!" Both boys' eyes widened as if they now had to communicate without words.

"Ha-ha, y'all got in trouble!" their two sisters sang in unison. Jacobie was the baby of the five siblings, and Jamica the second oldest behind Charlie. Ignoring the girls' taunt, the boys returned their focus to finding a pair of socks to use as a makeshift basketball.

"Okay, Shawn, you wanna play?" Charlie asked. "Then go find some socks."

Excited, Shawn took off running straight into the girls' bedroom.

"Nuh-uh!" Jamica yelled, chasing after her brother.

"Set 'em up! Set 'em up! Set they asses up!"

The commotion had all five kids running into the dining room, repeating, "Set 'em up, set 'em up!" Jacobie, never one to miss a chance to hit her solo, shouted, "Set they asses up," taking full advantage of being the baby who could get away with repeating swearwords.

"Why'd you count cut books?" asked Auntie Glorjean.

"Why'd you run trump takin all my cut books?" Auntie Red replied.

Fatty was also one of five siblings, but unlike her boys, she had only one brother. One by one, all five kids came and gave their mother hugs and kisses.

"Momma loves her babies!" said Fatty, with a loud kiss for each of them.

"We love you too, Momma!" they all replied.

"Come here, Nuka. They better let you play. Mwah, mwah! Extra kisses for Momma's baby!" she said.

"*I'm* baby!" exclaimed Jacobie as she tried to squeeze in.

"Yeah, Miss! Momma's baby needs to watch her mouth! Mwah! Mwah! All right, y'all go play—and let Nuka play too!" Nuka was the family nickname for Shawn, given to him by Fatty's cousin, Kim, who had passed away. Only Fatty called Shawn that, especially when she'd been drinking and was in a good mood.

"Let's set 'em up again, Fatty," Sobig whispered as the sisters' argument got louder. Sobig was a longtime family friend who'd grown up with the sisters.

"Nah, we switchin partners," Auntie Glorjean replied. "C'mon, Fatty!"

"Who's that knockin on the door, soundin like the po-lice?"

The kids were really into their basketball game; their balled-up socks couldn't bounce or dribble, but they still had fun shooting the "ball" toward their coat-hanger hoop. With the music playing and the younger girls cheerleading for their brothers, the knocking on the door went unnoticed.

"Hey, hey, why this door ain't locked?!" came a voice from outside. The kids, recognizing their father's voice, stopped playing and ran into the living room, shouting a chorus of "Daddy, Daddy, Daddy, Daddy, Daddy!"

"Come here to me, Daddy's babies!" Their father, DeAndre "Dre" Harris, started chasing the boys around the room. Dre was Charlie's idol. All the boys in the neighborhood looked up to Dre, even grown men did, but he was Charlie's father. Dre was the man. It went Michael Jordan then Dre. He even had attributes similar to Jordan's: athletic body and bald head. He'd once convinced a younger Charlie that he *was* the famous athlete. "Y'all seen me win my fourth championship!" Dre teased.

"Whatever, Michael Jordan!" Charlie said sarcastically, ashamed of the fact that he'd really believed it at one point.

Dre pulled out a wad of cash wrapped in a rubber band. "Who wants money?" He snapped the rubber band and began fingering through the bills in search of small denominations.

"I want money!" all five kids shouted. Dre gave each of them a twenty-dollar bill, but handed the biggest bill to his eldest.

"Why he gets the hundred-dollar bill?" asked a brokenhearted Jamica.

"Where my Fatty at?" Dre asked as he moved toward the dining room. Dre was the one who'd given Michelle the nickname—no one knew why, considering that she wasn't at all fat.

"You know the kids need clothes and supplies—the new school year is right around the corner," Fatty said, sipping an alcoholic drink.

"Shut up and make me one of those!" Dre demanded, tossing her a wad of cash. Dre and Fatty had broken off their engagement after Jacobie was born, deciding they were better at just coparenting. Looking like spies, Charlie and Jamica watched from around the corner, always hoping their mother and father would get back together.

The other women began at the same time: "Can I have some money too, Dre?"

"My car need fixin, Dre."

He pulled out his cash and handed each of them a hundred. This was one of the reasons why everyone loved Dre: he'd give you the shirt off his back if he fucked with you, but he'd put you in the ground quick if you messed with Fatty or the kids or got in the way of his hustle.

Dre turned and yelled toward the living room, "Kids! Grab your stuff, we goin to see Auntie Kat!"

Fatty looked at him and said, "How you gonna come in here actin like you the governor an' shit, passin out money and don't tell me you takin my kids to Chicago?"

"First of all, *our* kids, and second, you said they need school supplies. I remembered Kat paged me, told me she got them some school stuff."

"Well, I'm keepin this!" Fatty held up the wad of cash.

"Buy somethin special to wear. I'll be back" Dre replied in a suggestive tone. Sipping his own drink, he held her gaze.

"Y'all two need to just go ahead and get married!" all three women chimed in, breaking up the sexual tension.

On the way to Chicago to drop off the kids with Auntie Kat, who was Dre's mom's sister (and the kids' favorite Auntie), the kids got a chance to ride in one of their father's souped-up fancy cars. This one happened to be the '96 short-body Cadillac, which was almost as shiny as Dre's rings, chains, and watches. Gold rims, sound system, fresh paint job—dark blue with metallic flakes that made it sparkle like stars in the midnight sky. Charlie always got to sit in the front.

"Dad, can you teach me how to hustle?" Dre looked over at his son. "Ha, ha! This lil' nigga funny! 'How to hustle.' What you know bout hustlin?"

"I don't, that's why I want you to teach me," Charlie said.

"First off, we hustle 'cause we have to, but when you get your money right, then you can do what you wanna do! Second…"

"What's second, Dad?" asked Charlie.

"The hustle is classified! Ha-ha-ha-ha!"

Fourteen Years Later

Seattle, Washington, Charlie's 24th Birthday

"Damn! This seems hella hot."

"I told Possible never to meet in any type of secure room when making the exchange," Charlie says, as he and his younger brother, Shawn, take the elevator to the penthouse suite.

"Did he double-, triple-check to make sure who rented the suite is who they say they is?" asked Charlie.

"Chill, Charlie. I told you everythins good," Shawn replied.

"In and out, we count the money on the way in. I don't like this place," Charlie said as the elevator bell rang and the doors opened.

"Happy Birthday, Charlie!"

"Surprise, baby!" Charlie's high school sweetheart, Madeline Lopez, shouted as she kissed a confused Charlie on his lips.

"Where Possible?" asked Charlie

"Happy birthday, my nigga!" Possible yells as he pops a bottle of champagne. It's my nigga's twenty-fourth birthday, we gettin fucked up!"

"Come here!" Charlie said, grabbing Possible by the collar and giving him a tight hug.

"I love you, boy," Charlie whispered in Possible's ear as they embraced.

"I love you too," Possible whispered back.

Aight, aight! Enough of that soft shit," Shawn said. "It was my idea anyway," he added.

"Shut up!" Maddy and Possible shouted in unison.

Friends and family began to pay respects to Charlie.

"After everyone leaves I'll show you what I got for you," Maddy murmured seductively.

"Is that right?" Charlie replied in his own suggestive voice.

"That's right," Maddy said.

"Happy Birthday, Daddy!" yelled BJ, their three-year-old son, running into his father's arms.

"Boy, you gettin big. Pretty soon you'll be too heavy to pick up and carry around.

"I'll be big and strong like you?"

"Bigger and stronger than me," Charlie answered.

"Here's your present me and Mom got you." BJ handed his father a rectangular box. Maddy took BJ while Charlie opened it. "It's a Gucci tie," he says. "The same tie I was… I think we got a keeper." Maddy responded with a smile, kissed BJ on the cheek, and set him down. BJ went running through the room.

"I rented this suite for the weekend," Maddy said.

"Oh, you rented the suite, huh?" Charlie asked.

"Yeah, I did. You like it?" Maddy asked, sensing a hint of regret.

"I love it," Charlie replied.

"If you like it, I love it," Maddy said, kissing Charlie gently on the lips. Maddy began to go in for more, using her tongue this time. As she and Charlie began to kiss passionately, Maddy sensed something was bothering him.

"What's the matter?" she asked.

"I love the suite, but I gotta leave early morning."

"Why?" Maddy asked, disappointed.

"Work. One of our regulars is introducing us to new clientele."

"Have Shawn and Possible go," she said.

"That's like sending Possible by himself; Shawn can barely deal with our regulars."

"Ugh!" Maddy sighed. "We was supposed to go house shopping. I just picked out three beautiful houses to look at."

"Well, we can't get any of 'em if I don't work."

"How long will you be gone?"

"It's a few towns over, so a few hours' drive. I'll be back a li'l after midnight."

"Midnight!" Maddy snapped.

"Maybe before. Look, when I'm done we'll do it all, including doing it in this nice suite you got for my birthday."

"Shit, we doin it tonight!" Maddy responded excitedly. "Let's kick everybody out so we can get an early start."

"Party's over!" Charlie yelled.

They made passionate love all night, like it would be the last time they'd ever make love. Early the next morning Charlie's cellphone began to vibrate. Possible on the other end, letting Charlie know he was waiting down in the parking lot. Charlie took a shower, got dressed, and checked on BJ, who was sound asleep. Charlie kissed BJ on his forehead, then heard Maddy call for him. "Baby," she said, her voice groggy.

Charlie found her standing in the bedroom doorway in a bathrobe with nothing underneath it. They began to hug and kiss ardently! "Do you really have to leave now?" Maddy asked.

"I'll be back before you miss me," Charlie said.

"The thought of you having to leave makes me miss you already," Maddy replied. This put a smile on Charlie's face. Maddy always had a comeback line, for she truly loved Charlie as much as he loved her. Charlie gently kissed Maddy on the forehead. "I'll be back," he said.

"Love you," Maddy told him as he walked out the door.

"Top of the mornin," Possible greeted Charlie as he hopped into the car.

"You look like you had some good 'birthday cake,' huh!" Possible joked.

"Shut up and drive, let's get to the real cake," Charlie replied. As Possible pulled out of the parking lot, he began to update Charlie on the deal.

"So, Benny set up this move with these Russians who want twenty thousand pills."

"Twenty thousand on the first deal?" Charlie asked skeptically.

"They wanted fifty thousand, but I told 'em let's start small then work our way up."

"Where did Benny meet these Russians that could afford twenty thousand pills? He still owes on the hundred pack he picked up last week," Charlie said.

"I don't know, but I know what that means in profits," Possible shot back.

"Where's Benny now?" Charlie asked.

"He said he'd meet us there."

"Where's there?"

"Some crib in Milton. I got the address in the GPS. We good," Possible said, lighting up a blunt.

"Just think, my nigga, if we hit this joog once a month, or every other month, we wouldn't need any other joogs, period," Charlie replied.

"Yeah, yeah, mister corporate," Possible mocked, as he passed the blunt.

"I told you, Delvon got this clothing line that's startin to take off, and Shawn wanna get into the M.M.A." Charlie replied, inhaling a cloud of smoke.

"Shawn, M.M.A, that li'l nigga gonna get choked out fuckin wit them white boys," Possible said.

"All I'm sayin is we do this cause we got to, not cause we want to. When our paper right, then we do what we want to. Don't ever forget, my nigga," Charlie said.

"Anyways, the crib is in some rural area, like a construction site or somethin," Possible said, changing the subject.

"So how did Benny meet these Russians?" Charlie asked.

"I don't know," Possible replied. "You know Benny."

"That's the problem—I know Benny!" Charlie snapped. "Benny don't give a fuck bout nobody but Benny."

"You still trippin wit Benny? Remember, you pulled burner on Benny, not the other way round," Possible said.

"Remember, it's cause of you he's still alive," Charlie said.

"Benny's like family. He's just misunderstood."

"Or misfit," Charlie said.

"How much further we got to go?"

"GPS says two mins," Possible said, looking at his phone. He noticed a text from Benny. Possible put the phone on speaker as he waited for Benny to answer.

"Where y'all at?" Benny asked.

"We pullin up."

"I see you." Possible parked next to Benny as Benny hopped out of his car. Possible and Benny greeted each other, but Benny and Charlie just glanced at one another. Then the three started walking toward a house that looked like it was still being built.

"Charlie, it's been a while. Sorry I missed your party business," Benny said sarcastically.

"Dint know you got an invite," Charlie replied. The tension between the two was thick enough to cut with a knife."

"What's taking so long to answer the door?" Possible asked, breaking the awkward silence.

"Gentlemen," a burly bearded man with a heavy Russian accent greeted them. "I am Sasha. Follow me. Please excuse, how you Americans say, the mess. We still building. Welcome to Russia!"

The big man escorted them to a swanky kitchen with polished marble countertops and brand-new appliances. As if they couldn't be seen, two naked women were snorting lines of a crystalline substance off the shiny marble top.

"Don't mind my friends. They won't bite," Sasha teased.

"Not unless you want us to," one of the ladies said with a Russian accent, making eye contact with Charlie. An armed Russian stood in the hallway, guarding a closed bedroom door.

"Let's move to a more secure room, eh?" Sasha suggested.

"I don't like secure rooms. Why can't we do it here?" asked Charlie.

"What's the matter? We don't want everyone to know our business," Sasha replied. Charlie, Possible, and Benny followed him downstairs to a room where two big duffel bags lay on the floor.

"Three hundred fifty K in each bag, at thirty-five apiece, just like we agreed," said Sasha. Charlie looked at Possible, the signal to hand over the 20, 000 pills. Possible moved to toss the bag full of pills, but Benny intercepted it, pulled out a .40 caliber pistol, and aimed it at the Russian.

"I'll take that. Possible, grab the money!" Benny exclaimed.

"Benny, what the fuck are you doing?" Possible yelled, confused.

"What we doin is comin up, now grab the fuckin money!" snapped Benny.

"Benny, use your head, you think we'll get out of here alive?" Charlie asked calmly.

"Shut the fuck up, Charlie, nobody talkin to you! Far as I'm concerned you can stand next to Sasha," Benny said, aiming the pistol at Charlie.

"Hey, I'm the biggest meth distributor in America. Seven hundred K not much. Take it," the Russian said matter-of-factly.

Before he could say another word, two women pranced into the room. "Where's the party?" one asked, not grasping the situation. The other realized what was happening and began to scream, which gave Sasha the chance to pull and fire a small-caliber handgun. His shot missed Benny and hit Possible in the shoulder. Benny fired back, hitting Sasha in the arm.

As the women fled, the armed guard rushed in. Benny shot the man in the head. With him dead and Sasha wounded, Benny and Possible began to argue. "What the fuck, Benny, you fucked up. This wasn't—"

"Shut the fuck up!" Benny shouted. "I'm tired of being the third wheel all the time. You and—" Pow! Benny fell to the floor. Charlie held a .45, still aimed at where Benny's head had been when moments before he'd been standing.

"Let's go now!" Charlie said to Possible. Sasha, who lay bleeding on the floor, was cursing in Russian as the pair ran out of the room, up the stairs through the kitchen, and out the door. Possible was struggling to make it to the car, so Charlie helped him into the passenger seat and then slid behind the wheel.

"Ah, fuck! Mm, mm!" Possible moaned as they sped away from the scene.

"Where you hit?" Charlie asked calmly.

"The shoulder. I'll be aight."

"We gotta get you to the hospital."

Possible didn't reply. All he could think about was Benny's lifeless body hitting the floor.

"You killed Benny," he said with a blank stare.

"Benny was already dead," Charlie replied. "He just dint know it yet."

I'll Be Back Before You Miss Me

Charlie glanced in the rearview mirror and saw patrol lights flashing. As the two got to the freeway on-ramp, a state police car crossed the median and signaled Charlie to pull their vehicle over.

"Look," Charlie said, "Ima cop to everythin."

"No way—you'll never see the light of day. Wit no record, at least I got a chance," Possible said, struggling to sit up. "Plus, I'm shot—it's got self-defense all over this, they buy it."

Charlie sat in silence, thinking about his family, how he was supposed to go house hunting with Maddy, and how he would miss out on raising his only son. "Look, I'm responsible for this mess. You warned me. I shoulda never brought Benny's stupid ass into the mix. I got this."

Charlie knew that Possible had never been to prison, and he wasn't sure his friend could handle it, but Possible was right: with Charlie's record he'd be lucky if they didn't fry him. He pulled over. "I got you, bro!" he said, as a tear fell from his eye.

The state trooper yelled, "Driver, turn off the engine and toss your keys out the window—slowly!"

Chapter 2

Chain Day

Welcome to W.R.C. When I call your name, come up to the desk and grab a sack lunch and a bedroll," the big corrections officer yelled to the new Department of Corrections inmates as they waited to be processed into the system. "Blake, Caldwell, Daniels, Dempsey, Fernandez, Jenkins. … Jenkins! If I have to call your name one more time you're goin to the hole," the CO said.

Possible got his lunch and bedroll, then eyed his surroundings, awed by the fact that he would spend the next fifteen years in prison and that one of his best friends had killed his other best friend.

"Where you from, homie?" one of the Mexicans asked Possible.

"I'm from Elgin. Where you from?" Possible asked, confused—did this Mexican know him from somewhere?

"I from southside, homie!" the Mexican replied.

"Keep it moving, gentlemen. Do your homie stuff in the yard," the CO said in an irritated tone, then continued to call inmates: "Sanders, Sanchez, Washington, Williams."

"Ese, this my partner. He good. Who you, *vato?*" the Mexican asked.

"I'm Sweaty, from the city, homie," Deon "Sweaty" Washington said.

"What you fools wanna do?" another Mexican yelled as he walked up to the group of three. Possible was utterly confused by now, but understood that it was about to go down, so before Sweaty could reply, Possible threw a right hook to the Mexican's jaw, catching him off guard. Before the man touched the ground, Sweaty had already swung, connecting with the chin of the second Mexican. A third jumped in, then a fourth, and before Possible and Sweaty knew it, they were fighting with their backs to each other.

"Stop fighting! Stop fighting and get on the ground, now!" COs came running from all directions, Mace in hand, and sprayed without regard for the inmates' eyes. The chemical quickly took its toll, and all six men went down.

"That's right. Sweaty from the city. Anytime you want it, let me know!" Sweaty shouted, face full of Mace, smiling and coughing as two COs struggled to stand him up.

Possible couldn't understand why the Mexicans had a problem with him. As he and Sweaty were escorted to the hole, the prison went on lockdown.

* * *

"Whoa, this shit burns!" Sweaty exclaimed as he showered off the Mace. "Ay, what's your name, homie? Sweaty pounded on the shower wall to get Possible's attention. "Homie, what's your name?"

"Possible!"

"Who?"

"Possible!" Just as he shouted over the sound of the water, the showers cut off.

"Why they call you Possible?" Sweaty asked, lowering his voice.

"Doctor told my mom it was impossible to have a kid, so she nicknamed me Possible."

"Thas what's up. I'm Sweaty, from the city!"

"Yeah, I got that back there," Possible replied sarcastically. "What's up with the Mexicans?"

"Look," Sweaty said. You got Southsiders, Northsiders, and Paisas. Those were Southsiders. They don't get along with Blacks," he explained. "Where you from?"

"Elgin, IL," Possible said.

"Naw, like, what you bang?"

"I don't bang. I get money."

"Ay, my guy say he gets money," Sweaty mocked, laughing. Where'd you fall out of?" he asked.

"Milton, but I live in Kirkland," Possible said. "Where all the rich white people live."

"Well, I can tell you never been to prison, so just follow my lead and keep servin it how you did back there in intake!"

* * *

After six months in the hole, and having to start orientation over, Possible and Sweaty were transferred to a maximum facility where they were assigned to the same unit but different pods. "Where you goin?" asked Sweaty.

"H unit, Pod 2," Possible said with a smile, happy to be out of the hole.

"Fuck, they split us up. I'm goin to Pod 3," Sweaty replied. "It's all good, just put a kite in to the unit sergeant. Tell 'im you're my cousin and we wanna cell up. Ima do it too."

Putting a kite to anybody was the last thing on Possible's mind, and besides, he'd just spent six months in the hole next door to Sweaty, so a break from him wouldn't be so bad. It'd been almost seven months now that Possible had been in prison, and he'd heard nothing from Charlie. He'd tried calling, but the number had been changed, and his letters came back marked

Return to Sender. Possible had known Charlie since he was nine years old, and this was the first time he'd ever questioned Charlie's loyalty. It crushed him, and it made him feel guilty.

He thought about calling GG. "Hello, Grandma," Possible said when she accepted the call.

"Hey, baby, what took you so long to call me?" she asked.

"They just gave me back my property, wit your number in my phonebook," Possible said.

"Why they take so long to give my baby his property?"

"Long story. I, uh, I—"

"Long story? Well, you got time, tell me what happen. You know you can tell me if they messin wit you in there."

"Naw, GG, nobody messin wit me," Possible replied with a smile.

"You know yo brother been waitin for you to call. He gave me a number to give you."

Charlie and Possible weren't blood related, but GG had always considered Possible family.

"Charlie?" he asked, pleased.

"Yeah. Wait, let me get it. You know he went to jail. Them peoples had him and Maddy out there fightin, and somebody called the po-lice. Charlie got out last week, askin if you called. He said don't tell you, but you know Grandma don't keep secrets from her babies."

"What peoples had them fightin?"

"I don't know y'all friends. He said call him." GG gave Possible the phone number.

"Outside of that, how you doin? I—"

"GG, I gotta go!"

"You just called for Charlie. You dint wanna speak to me," GG snapped back.

"Naw, GG, but I don't got a lot of time. I love you. Call you soon."

"Love you too, baby."

It'd been a week since Possible had gotten Charlie's new number from GG. He'd been excited, but now he was nervous. He wasn't sure if Charlie had forgotten about him. After all, it had been Possible's idea to take the blame for everything. Charlie wasn't obligated, and besides, Possible felt that if their roles were reversed, Charlie would have done the same for him.

"Check or bet. Check or bet, nigga. It's on you, Possible," one of the poker players said.

"I'm all in," Possible snapped.

"Call," Matt said.

Possible turned his hand over and showed three tens.

"Sorry, my nigga. Maybe next time get your head in the game. You down a hundred 'n' fifty," Matt said.

"I got you. I need to use the phone," Possible replied in a defeated tone.

"Yeah, we know, and put mines on my media—you still got my info, right? Shit, you should know it by heart." Matt yelled as Possible ran to the phone. Possible wasn't worried about putting money on Matt's media right this minute; he knows he's got the money, and he knows Matt, but he just decided to call Charlie.

The robot voice said, "You have a prepaid call from… Possible. You will not be charged for this call. To accept this call press 5 now. Thank you."

Charlie answered the phone. "Peety!" That was the name Charlie and Possible called each other. Charlie gave Possible that nickname because his first name was Pierre, and Possible called Charlie Peety cause he had a peanut-shaped head.

"Peety!" Possible said back. "Man, what's good? Bro, I been goin through it," Possible said, rubbing his head.

"What happen?" asked Charlie, concerned.

"Naw, I just got off the chain. The Mexicans got to beefin wit me and this nigga name Sweaty, me and him got 'em up wit four of 'em," Possible explained.

"You good?" Charlie asked.

"I did my thang. I tried writin and I got the letter returned to sender. Sabrina said you disappeared, I was in the hole like 'No way, not my nigga.'"

"Naw," Charlie said. "I been lightweight goin through it too. Me and Maddy got into it wit some niggas at the apartments, and police showed up and took me in for DV (domestic violence). They wouldn't give me bail. They tryna put a restrainin order on me and Maddy, but we gettin it dropped after these classes," he explained.

"Got my nigga takin classes, huh?" Possible replied.

"Look, Maddy said she put two hundred on your books. She also ordered shoes, TV, watch, hotpot, JP5 player, all the shit and stuffses. Oh, and I put money on the phone, on my phone and your pin.

"I appreciate you," Possible replied.

"I told you," Charlie said. "I got you. Don't even trip. My bad bout all this shit. We gonna be straight, so you can hit me anytime."

"How's everythin lookin out there wit the family business?" Possible asked.

"I mean, you know, shit still coolin off after everythin, so our regulars kinda spooked cause the Russians killed Benny," Charlie explained.

The Russians, Possible thought. He'd just realized that Charlie hadn't told the real about how everything had gone down, either that or he hadn't wanted to talk over a recorded phone call.

"Yeah, I told Factor and everybody else it's good, but they wanna wait to see what happ—"

"You have sixty seconds remaining," the animated voice interrupted.

"Aight, Peety," Possible said.

"I got you, my nigga. Don't trip. Ima handle everythin out here, you just stay out the way and leave them Mexicans alone."

"You have thirty seconds remaining."

"Aight, bro, Ima hit you in a few days. Love you, bro."

"Aight. Love you too. Keep yo head up, one," Charlie replied before the phone cut off.

Possible hung up, relieved that Charlie was all right and they're good, but now Possible had more questions than answers about the family business and how everything would turn out. He hadn't taken this bid for Charlie to stop taking care of the family business. *If that's the case, bring yo ass to prison and I'll handle everythin.* In his heart he knew Charlie would make it happen and take care of business.

"Ay, Matt. My bro said he put two hundred on my books, but I only got ninety." Checking the balance on his inmate account, Matt cracked a smile. "You should have less than that if you put the hundred fifty on my media like I told you!" Matt teased.

He checked Possible's account balance on the kiosk, a self-service touch-screen system where inmates can access their account history, place commissary orders, and see facility bulletins and information.

"Yeah, yeah, whatever," Possible replied with a smirk.

"They take fifty-five percent from you for LFOs—legal financial obligations—savings, and cost of confinement, but it could be worse, they take ninety-five percent off me," Matt explained. "Matter of fact, just order thirty dollars in store and put thirty on my media. Ima make my store list tonight," he said.

"Whatever," Possible said again. "Let's get a table started now."

"We gotta wait till everybody get back from school and work, and we bout to lock down in fifteen minutes," Matt said.

"Inmate Jenkins to the sergeant's office!" the dayroom intercom announced.

"You heard 'im, Jenkins," Matt joked, assuming it meant Possible was in trouble.

Chapter 3

P.T.S.D

"Mr. Jenkins, have a seat. I'm the unit sergeant, Mr. Jackson. I been receiving kites about a Washington wanting to cell up with you," he said.

"Yeah, I forgot to put a kite in."

"No worries. That's why you're here, to make sure you guys are on the same page. You know this is a ninety-day commitment?" Sergeant Jackson asked.

"Yeah, I know," Possible said.

"All right. It'll be either this week or next week. I got a bunch of moves to do, so I'll take care of it ASAP. You make sure not to go getting into trouble with Mr. Washington. I haven't heard your name, which is a good thing, but I'm all too familiar with Washington," Jackson said.

"It won't be a problem, sir. I'll keep him out of trouble," Possible said with a smile.

"All right, I'm gonna hold you to that," Jackson replied.

On the way back to the cell, Possible was having second thoughts about celling up with Sweaty. After all, he'd just met him and had already been in a riot, and Sergeant Jackson expected Possible to stick to his word! The thought came that Sweaty was trying to help Possible. *Can't be too much worse than the cellie I have now*, he thought.

"On the fuckin ground, now! Jenkins, get on the ground! COs rushed into the unit. Possible turned to see five guards run past him into the dayroom. Because he was in the unit sally port, a secure doorway designed to prevent any unwanted entry or exit, he couldn't see what was going on. All he knew was some type of fight was happening.

COs yelled, "Break it up now! Stop fighting!"

Anxious to see what was doing. Possible began to belly crawl out of the sally port. From his new vantagepoint he could see two white boys on the ground, one bleeding profusely from the neck and the other being cuffed, a huge smirk on his face.

"Move out the way!" medical staff shouted as they brought a stretcher into the dayroom.

"Lockdown! Get to your fuckin cells, now! Lockdown!"

Possible hurried to his feet as the guards began to give orders. "Don't walk through here. Go the other way!" Another CO barked at Possible as he tried to make it to his cell. Walking back, Possible stared in awe at all the blood on the floor. At that moment, he had a flashback to the incident with the Russians. Benny's brains blown out the side of his skull, his body falling to the floor, blood flowing from a huge hole in his head.

"Jenkins! Jenkins!" Office Peters yelled, then grabbed Possible and cuffed him up. Possible was still in shock. Within the past eighteen months he had been around more dead bodies than he'd ever seen before. Charlie had always tried to shield Possible from this side of things, understanding that if you weren't mentally tough it could have negative effects.

"The fuck you doin, Benny?!"

"I'm tired of bein the third wheel. You and—" POW! Possible jolted out of a deep sleep.

"Ay, homie, 10-10, keep it down over there!" Possible's neighbor yelled.

"We in the hole, ain't no such thing!" another inmate yelled out his cell door. *The hole again,* Possible thought. "What time is it?" he shouted.

"Four ay em! Now be quiet!"

Possible climbed back into his bunk and stared at the ceiling, thinking about the last year and half compared to the previous twenty. How did everything turn for the worse so soon, and so bad? He was finally hearing Charlie's voice, how this was not the lifestyle he wanted them to live.

"We do this cause we have to, not cause we want to. When our paper right, then we do what we want to." Charlie's voice echoed in Possible's head. He rolled over, closed his eyes, and tried to sleep.

"Jenkins! Jenkins! Pack it up, you're back to the unit. Get ready, they're coming to get you in ten minutes," a female CO ordered Possible through the cell intercom. On the walk back to the unit, Possible was thinking about his off-and-on girlfriend Sabrina. Maybe a visit from her would be what he needed to bounce back.

"Look at this guy! Boy, what's wrong wit you? Matt asked Possible as he entered the dayroom.

"Talk to me, my nigga. You were like a deer in the headlights. Aight, it's all good, we ain't gotta talk right now. Ima let you settle in," Matt said as he walked away.

Sweaty greeted possible as the cell door opened. "What's good, my nigga?" Possible just pushed past him without a word.

"Damn, my nigga, don't be like that," Sweaty said. "I told 'em I'd wait to move in till you got out the hole. Look, I even made you a cheesecake. CO Peters told me you was comin back today."

"Not right now, Sweaty. It's got nothin to do wit you," Possible replied somberly.

"Look, my nigga, I know how hard yo first bid can be, 'specially when you're not from any hood, but I got you." Sweaty held up a joint with a smile.

"What's that?" Possible asked in a disinterested tone.

"Here, finish makin your bed, get yourself settled, and Ima put this together.

It looks like it's already together, said Possible, examining the stick and realizing it was marijuana.

"Yeah, but I gotta get the lighter ready," Sweaty replied with a smile. "We gonna spark on the next walk."

Just as Possible finished settling in, CO Peters exited the unit after a tier check.

"You do the honors," Sweaty said, handing Possible the stick as he popped the socket for the fire. Possible could hear the buds roasting as he took a hard toke on the stick.

"Damn, my nigga, this ain't no blunt!" Sweaty complained. I wanna smoke too," he said, grabbing the stick. "You tap it," he demonstrated, passing the stick back to Possible.

"There you go, tap it, go 'head, kill it," Sweaty said.

Possible was all too familiar with this feeling; everything that had taken place in a year and a half now felt like a thing of the past—exactly what Possible needed. A soothing feeling flowed through him.

"Ay, bro, you whippin!" Sweaty said.

Possible started blankly at the TV as if it were on.

"Possible!" Sweaty yelled.

"What!" Possible snapped.

"First of all, don't get stuck. Remember you're in prison. Weed is illegal. Second, don't 'what?' me," Sweaty said as he poked Possible in the forehead.

Possible smiled and got up in a boxing stance.

"Square up, then," Sweaty said with a smile, getting into his own stance. The two began to slap box, then started wrestling. Possible got Sweaty in a choke hold.

"Aight, aight!" Sweaty yelled as he tapped out of it.

"Understand the peckin order—you're the li'l homie," Possible said, squeezing and laughing.

"I can't breathe!" Sweaty struggled to get out of the hold.

"Aight!" Possible said and let him go.

"Damn, you tryna blow my high, you payin for the next one," Sweaty exclaimed.

Exhausted, he struggled to breathe while lying on his back in the middle of the cell floor. Equally exhausted, Possible sat on his bunk, proud of himself, thinking that moving Sweaty in had been the right decision.

"Where's that cheesecake," Possible asked with a smile.

Chapter 4

My Voice Matters

The next morning, a CO's voice over the unit's intercom woke the inmates for breakfast: "IDs on, shirts tucked in, mainline Pod 2, last call, mainline Pod 2!"

Sweaty had been up an hour earlier watching *First Take*, a sports debate show. "See, if you *stay* ready, you don't have to *get* ready," he said, as Possible rushed to brush his teeth and wash his face.

"Where's my ID?" Possible asked.

"Clipped to the shelf, where it's gonna be every mornin, so get used to it." Sweaty replied.

"Ay, you ready?" Possible asked before pushing the button.

"I stay ready."

"Yeah, yeah, so you don't ha' to get ready," Possible mocked as the cell door popped open.

"Ay, top of the mornin," Matt announced, smiling at Possible and Sweaty.

"Top of the mornin," they replied in unison. As the three walked to the chow hall together, they talked about last night's basketball game between Lebron and Durant, a topic Matt loved to debate, especially if Lebron was involved.

"Man, Durant is the best player in the world," Sweaty snapped at Matt as he reached for his breakfast tray.

"You gotta be smokin rock if you think Durant better than Lebron. Durant ain't even better than James Harden," Matt snapped back.

"What?!" Oh, hell no, you can't talk basketball no more. Lemme get this straight, you rather have James Harden then Kevin Durant? Sweaty asked, a disgusted look on his face.

"You heard me. I don't got to worry bout James Harden jumpin ship if we lose in the playoffs," Matt replied as they took their seats at the table where two other Black inmates, J-money and Li'l D, were already eating.

"You hear what this adolescent just said?" asked Matt.

Li'l D looked up with a smile and shook his head no. "But I can hear y'all arguin from the breezeway."

"This nigga said Durant the best player in the world, over Lebron James."

Matt eyed J-money as if to say, *Can you believe this?*

"But this dinosaur say he rather have James Harden than Durant," Sweaty replied with a facial expression that said *I smell shit.*

"This what you dealin wit early this mornin?" J-money asked Possible.

"That's why I don't watch sports," Possible replied, stuffing his mouth full of oatmeal.

"Oh, hell, no!" Sweaty said.

"Somethings wrong with you," Matt said, pointing at Possible.

"Ay, on a serious tip, Dam'on wants niggas in the yard this afternoon!" J-money announced in a low tone.

"Dam'on always tryna call meetins and shit." Matt said with a frown. "I guess it's bout the white boy gettin poked and Possible goin to the hole durin that."

"Me goin the hole, I had nothin to do wit that," said Possible.

"We know that, but word is you poked 'im."

"If I poked 'im, why they let me out the hole?"

"I know—I'm just the messenger, passin along the message," J-money replied.

"Don't even trip, we'll be there," Sweaty said, smiling at Possible.

"Shit I was tryna sit back and watch my soaps this afternoon," Matt replied.

"That the problem right there, them damn soaps, talkin bout you rather have Harden than Durant," Sweaty answered with that *I smell shit* face.

"Y'all niggas be easy. We'll see y'all at the yard," Li'l D said, smiling at Sweaty's facial expression as he and J-money excused themselves from the table.

"Don't trip bout Dam'on wantin to talk to you. It's coo," Sweaty assured Possible.

"Yeah, if you wanna be in the mix," Matt butted in. "I don't know if I'm goin."

"Okay, and…," Sweaty replied.

"See, you always gotta say somethin smart," Matt answered as he got up from the table, leaving Possible and Sweaty.

"I got your back if them nigga on some funny shit," Sweaty assured Possible." If *who* on some funny shit?" Zay said, sitting down at the table with I Like It Here.

"Oh, shit, what's good, my nigga?" Sweaty embraced the two men with their own handshake. "Ay, these are my niggas from my hood, Zay and I Like It Here," Sweaty said.

"This who you left us for, huh?" Zay replied.

Greeting the two men, Possible said, "They call me Possible."

CO Hunter broke in: "Washington, you and your friend tray up, let's go."

"Aight, we outta here, go to yard, "Sweaty said.

"Yep!" Zay responded.

"Let's go, Mr. Washington!" CO Hunter demanded a second time. "Damn, Ms. Hunter, ain't you look nice today," Sweaty said.

"Out, Mr. Washington," CO Hunter replied. Then, with a seductive smile directed at Possible, she said, "I strongly suggest you find someone else to hang out with."

"Don't be like that… with your fine ass," Sweaty replied, but saved the *with your fine ass* part till after they'd walked out of the chow hall.

"Who was that?" Possible asked with excitement.

"That Ms. Hunter. She been married to three different COs, got no kids, rumor has it she can't have any," Sweaty said.

"She's thick as fuck," Possible said.

"You like white girls, huh?"

"I don't know, white blondes just do somethin to me."

As the two made it back to their cell, Sweaty decided to break down the politics of closed custody. "So Matt never pulled you up on how shit goes round here?" he asked.

"Naw, not really."

"Aight, look: H unit is pretty laid-back, but down in J unit they politic hard—showers, tables, yard, and phones are segregated. The whites and Southsiders share, and the Blacks and API and Natives share. All them other guys run their cars different than we do. We hardheaded, we answer to nobody, but we try to hold each other accountable. No City G is gonna take orders from no Burgundy B or Royal C, and vice versa, so where there's a problem with one of the City G's we handle it. When there's a problem wit Burgundy B, then the B's handle it. Same wit Royal C's. Now, if an outsider, meaning non-Black or from a different car, got a problem, then we all got a problem, G's, C's, and B's.

"That sounds pretty simple," Possible replied.

"Yeah, but it gets complicated when we don't communicate and we not on the same page. That's why Dam'on wants us on the yard."

"Where's Dam'on from?" Possible asked.

"Dam'on from Burgundy B's," Sweaty said. The, in air quotes, added, "He speaks for the Blacks."

"Why the air quotes?" Possible asked.

"cause I speak for myself. You know some niggas don't have a voice and some don't even matter," Sweaty said.

"Shit, mines matter," Possible said under his breath.

"What? I couldn't hear you."

"Mines matter!" Possible replied louder.

"Aight, let me know it, then."

"Oh, before I forget, what's up wit I Like It Here," Possible asked.

"That homie's just institutionalized, he been in the system his entire life. At his sentencin he told the judge, 'I like it here,' and that's been his handle ever since."

"The judge game him life?"

"Naw, sixty-five years."

Over the intercom, CO Peters yelled, "H-unit, prepare for yard! H-unit, yard!"

Possible didn't know what to expect, but understood one thing: his voice mattered.

Chapter 5

Bend A Lap With Me

"I thought you had to catch soaps," Sweaty said, teasing Matt. "Somebody gotta be the voice of reason." Matt replied, smiling at Possible. As the three entered the yard, Possible noticed the tension immediately. He'd been to the yard a few times, and could tell that this yard had a different feel. Nobody but two older Blacks working out, everybody else grouped up by race, talking relaxedly amongst themselves.

"Sweaty! Over here!" Zay yelled from the crowd of Blacks.

"Shit wit y'all Black mothafuckas piled up like this. We can see y'all from the unit talkin bout some over here," Matt joked, shaking everybody's hand. As the last of the Blacks made their way to the group, greeting each other with handshakes and finding their places—Burgundy B's, Royal C's, and the City G's and a few neutral Blacks—Dam'on began to speak.

"Aight, Aight, I ain't gonna be long, you know they watchin us"

At that, all the guards in the yard, including the guard in the gun tower, observed the group closely.

"I just wanted everybody in H-unit on the same page—the white boy incident had nothing to do with us. Niggas down in J-unit thought it did because one of the Blacks went to the hole during that situation, but it was for a different reason, so when y'all go back to work and school Monday, let 'em know," said Dam'on.

"Who went to the hole?" someone from the Royal C's asked.

"It don't matter, he's already out the hole," Dam'on replied.

Blacks from Burgundy B's and Royal C's started whispering and pointing to the City G's

"What the fuck y'all whisperin and pointin at?" yelled Sweaty. "My nigga went to the hole for somethin else. Y'all got a problem wit that?" he asked.

Zay and I Like It Here stood up from the benches they were seated on, and a few other City G's stopped their side conversations. The City G's were the smallest of the three cliques, but you couldn't tell them that in this moment.

"We just wanted to make sure he's good, that's all," some guy from Royal C's shot back.

Everyone seemed to shake their heads in agreement.

Breaking the awkward silence that followed, Matt yelled, "Well, since we all agreein and shit, let's agree to break this shit up!"

"Aight, Black men!" Dam'on yelled, ending the meeting. The group dispersed, catching up with those from other pods to share the latest gossip.

"Possible bend a lap wit me?" Dam'on asked Possible who was talking to Sweaty and Zay.

"What's good?" asked Possible in a "for what?" manner.

Matt began, "Bring yo peanut—"

Possible interrupted, "We talked bout that already."

Matt just smiled, as the two, Possible and Dam'on started to walk around the yard.

"I'm Dam'on, homie."

"Possible."

"Nice to meet you," Dam'on said as he shook Possible's hand.

"You're not from City G's?" asked Dam'on, wondering why Possible didn't do the City G handshake.

"Naw, I don't bang, I get money," Possible replied.

Dam'on smiled. "Where you from?"

"Elgin, outside of Chicago," Possible said.

"Yep. I had some work out there in Rockford and Aurora," Dam'on said. "What city you fall out of?"

"Milton, but I lived in Kirkland, Bellevue area," Possible answered.

"I'm from Eastside of Tacoma. Look, homie, I want you to know that we got each other backs down here. I heard the situation shook you up a li'l bit, but none of that matters. I heard bout the situation with the Mexicans back at W.R.C. I heard nothing but good things bout you, so that dint match up wit what I hear of the unit situation."

"Naw, I been dealing wit some personal shit from my case. Kinda got stuck, that's all."

"Yep. Anytime you wanna pop it, let me know. I'm in Pod 3. You got everythin?"

"I'm straight," Possible said.

"Here, take this." Dam'on spat out two pieces of plastic, wiped them off on his shirt, then handed them to Possible. "Sweaty your cellie, right?"

"Yep."

"Aight, that's my nigga, he wit the business. Don't let him drive, though," Dam'on said.

"Aight." Possible had no idea what Dam'on meant by "Don't let him drive," but instead of asking, at the risk of looking stupid, he just thanked Dam'on.

"Good lookin. I appreciate it." Possible said, and walked off toward Matt.

* * *

"We gonna get a table started tonight at dayroom," Matt announced with a grin as Possible walked up to him.

"You know I'm ready," Possible replied.

"This time, when you lose, just shoot those two sticks Dam'on shot you," said Matt.

Confused, Possible asked, "How did you know?"

From the gun tower, the CO shouted through his bullhorn, "Yard Closed! Yard in! Line up on the fence! Yard Closed!"

Chapter 6

Shoot Your Shot

"Top of the mornin," Sweaty said to Possible without breaking focus on *First Take*, his favorite sports show.

"Damn, my nigga, is that shit that good?" Possible asked as he took a piss.

"Mr.'I Don't Like Sports,' don't interrupt one's study," Sweaty replied sarcastically.

"Oh, yeah, I guess I'll just face these two sticks then. I wouldn't wanna interrupt your studies," Possible teased as he washed his hands and began to roll one of the sticks.

"Ay, man, where you get that?" Sweaty asked, finally making eye contact.

"One shall not interrupt when one is rollin, Possible teased.

"That's not what I asked you."

"Don't worry bout where it came from, worry bout where it's goin," Possible shot back as he put the final touches on the stick. "Get the flame ready," he ordered.

"On the next commercial," answered Sweaty.

"What?"

"We gotta wait on the next walk anyway. I seen Ms. Hunter doing count earlier too," Sweaty added.

"No you dint, cause she don't work in the units.

"She does today," Sweaty said.

Possible had the biggest grin on his face. At that moment they heard the unit door open.

"Here she comes right now," Sweaty yelled with excitement.

Possible jumped off the bunk so fast that he lost his footing and fell headfirst into the cell door.

"Ha-ha-ha-ha-ha!" Sweaty burst into laughter and dropped to the floor, tears rolling down his cheeks. Choking and coughing, barely able to breathe, he held his stomach.

"You play too much!" Possible snapped, rubbing his aching head. "That's aight. I got you. That was funny, huh?" he asked, smiling at the image in his mind of himself falling.

"You guys all right in here?" As he passed by, CO Vasquez heard the commotion and saw Sweaty on the floor, holding his stomach.

"We good, Vasquez." Sweaty was barely able to get the words out from laughing so hard.

CO Vasquez start to examine the cell, surveying Possible and Sweaty for any of signs of trouble, but concluded the two were just guff-balls.

"No more guffing off, you two." Vasquez warned and walked off.

"I facin this stick," snapped Possible.

"Ooh, shit, this nigga damn near broke his neck for that rat," Sweaty teased. The unit door closed and Possible sparked immediately.

"My nigga, if you feel like that, shoot your shot," Sweaty suggested.

"Don't worry bout all that, Ima shoot when I shoot," Possible replied, inhaling a cloud of smoke.

"Oh, really, gonna face the whole stick, huh?"

Possible smiled. "Here, my nigga. I'm just fuckin wit you," he said, passing the stick.

"Where you get this from?" asked Sweaty inhaling smoke.

"Dam'on."

"I knew that," Sweaty said, exhaling the cloud.

"You know Dam'on's the guy; he got shit sold up both units," Sweaty said, visibly conflicted on passing the roach to Possible.

"Go 'head and kill it," Possible said.

Possible was in deep thought about his conversation with Dam'on. He liked Dam'on, liked how the brother carried himself, with a special type of aura about him—humble, levelheaded, and very aware of how others felt and thought.

"I like Dam'on," Possible said.

"I knew you would. I told you Dam'on coo. How many sticks he give you?" Sweaty asked.

"Two."

"Two?"

"Yeah, two, dammit!" Possible replied loudly.

"That's one cheap-ass nigga."

"My Nigga, he don't owe us anything, he not obligated to give us anything," Possible said.

"Aight. I'm just saying he got hella that shit, two sticks ain't nothin."

"That's two more'n he had to give us."

"Y'all ain't comin out?" Matt interrupted, catching them off guard as he popped up at their cell door.

"We dint even hear them call dayroom," Sweaty replied pushing the button to open the cell door.

"You got lucky last night," Matt told Possible, in reference to the poker game the night before. "Let's get a table started," he suggested. "I can see those sticks are gone," he added.

Sweaty smiled at Matt to confirm that.

"You had your shot last night and you blew it," Possible exclaimed.

"I couldn't catch a hand for shit," snapped Matt, thinking about how he was supposed to be up two sticks.

"I gotta use the phone 'fore we start. I'll be back," Possible told them as he made his way to the phone. He thought about calling Sabrina, but decided to call Charlie instead.

Charlie answered, "Peety!" What's happenin?"

"I been waitin on you to call, tell you that Sabrina and Maddy comin to visit you.

"When?" Possible asked, excited.

"Today. They left early this morning, round four ay em. They should be close if not there already."

"Oh, shit, they call visits in an hour. I gotta go shower, get dressed, but my hair, all the shit and stuffses."

"Yup, hit me when you get out the visit. Ay, did—"

Possible hung up the phone before Charlie could finish his question. This was the first visit Possible had had since he'd been in prison, and he's been thinking about Sabrina a lot lately.

"Ay, I'm bout to deal you in!" Matt yelled as Possible ran through the dayroom.

"Naw, I got a visit," Possible shouted back. "If I can get my cell door open," he added, trying to get the attention of the booth officer.

"Aight, have a good one," Sweaty yelled.

The cell door began to open, and Possible rushed in to get ready. Ten minutes later, the booth officer alerted Possible of his visitors.

"Jenkins!"… Jenkins!"

"Yeah!"

"You got a visit!" the officer announced over the intercom.

"Possible wanted to say, *Yeah, I know. If you dint take forever to open my door I'd be ready by now!* Instead he said, "Here I come!"

"Push the button when you're ready."

Possible's personal property still hadn't arrived, but he always kept a brand-new pair of state-issued shoes, creased jeans, and some fresh white tees.

"Jenkins!" You got two minutes or you're gonna have to catch the next gate." At this moment Possible stumbled out of the cell, his pants falling, trying to lotion his face, grease his hair, and get his belt through the loops of his pants all at the same time.

"Damn, you need help?" Sweaty offered. Possible jerked away in irritation.

"I'm good, good lookin, though."

"Where's your ID?" asked Sweaty.

"Fuck!"

"Go. I'll grab it," Sweaty said.

"It's on my old shirt on the floor," Possible yelled as he walked through the unit door into the sally port. While Sweaty waited to get the cell open, the booth officer came over the intercom: "Washington, you go in, you stay in!"

"My cellie forgot his ID."

"Hurry up!"

Sweaty runs in grabs the ID off the shirt on the floor and finds a stick lying next to it. *Wow, this guy is trippin*, Sweaty thought. He ran to catch the group of guys on their way to visit.

"Here, you slippin too!" Sweaty said with attitude.

"Good lookin," Possible answered, without regard for Sweaty's *You're slippin* comment.

"Have a good one, bro," Sweaty replied with a smile.

Still fixing himself as he hustled out the unit door and headed toward the breezeway, he spotted Dam'on rushing toward the visiting building. Possible immediately put two and two together as he himself entered.

Chapter 7

All the Shit and Stuffses

"Gentlemen, IDs in the box and move into the holding cell," the visiting officer ordered as the inmates begin to file in. Another officer appeared. "All right, come out two at a time for pat-down search."

The men began to come out as ordered.

"Possible, what's good?" Dam'on asked as the two moved to the back of the line.

"Finally get to see my girl" Possible replied eagerly.

"That's what's up? Have a good one," said Dam'on.

"Yep, you too."

As the door to the visiting room opened, it was like a bright light at the end of a dark tunnel. There were so many people in the room that it was hard for Possible to find his visitors.

"Baby! Oh, my God!" Sabrina shouted. Unable to find her face, but recognizing her voice, Possible found Sabrina and Maddy buying food at the vending machines.

"I got this, girl," Maddy said to Sabrina as she went skipping across the room.

"Oh, baby!" Possible hugged Sabrina so tight he could hear her back crack. They began to kiss passionately.

"I dint' know y'all was comin. I called Charlie an hour ago and he said y'all was on the way. I had to hurry and get ready," Possible said as the two took their seats.

"Oh, baby, you look so good. I can tell you was rushin—you missed a spot on your chin strap. You still look good though. Why haven't you been checkin your emails on Jpay. I sent you pics and told you a week in advance me and Maddy was comin," Sabrina said.

"Man, I'm still settlin in. I don't check Jpay cause it be long lines and a lot of drama over the Jpay. I dint know you knew how to use it, but I got you."

"No, I got you, baby." Sabrina shot back, grabbing Possible's hand. They stared into each other eyes without speaking, basking in the moment.

"What's up, Possible?" Maddy asked, breaking the ambiance, both arms filled with plates of food.

"Damn, Maddy, let me help you. You like a waitress with them plates stacked on your arms like that.

"Did you forget what I do for a living?" Maddy asked as she set the plates on the table.

"Where's my hug at?" Possible gave Maddy a hug and proceeded to eat.

"I was just telling him I sent pics and emails bout us comin up a few weeks ago," Sabrina said to Maddy.

"I dint know she knew how to use Jpay," Possible replied defensively through a mouthful of food.

"I showed her how to do everythin Jpay: put money on your books, order packages for you, look up your visiting schedule, put money on the phone—

"All the shit and stuffses," Possible interrupted.

"When Charlie was locked up the first time, I used to be able to order clothes and shoes, but they stopped that years ago," Maddy said, grabbing a buffalo wing.

"Speaking of Charlie," Sabrina chimed in, "He's upset wit you. He said you don't call or email him back."

"He got a Jpay too?"

"Jpay is the shit—I can send emails and you'll get them the same day," Maddy said.

"Man, I should have known, cause guys be fightin and arguin over Jpay; they be payin for spots in line, and now I see why."

"Did you get your tablet and shoes? How bout all your personal property?" Sabrina asked.

"Naw, I dint get nothin yet."

"No TV?"

"My cellie got a TV, hot pot, all the shit and stuffses.

"Yeah, but I want my baby to have his own stuff," Sabrina said, squeezing Possible's hand affectionately.

"I told you, girl, that it could take a minute. I told you to track it, right?" Maddy asked Sabrina.

"Yeah, Ima look it up when I get home."

"What you be doin in here, baby?" Sabrina asked.

"Man, I been goin through it a li'l bit, gettin used to how shit operates round here. I got into a riot first day I got in the joint."

"You told me bout that," Sabrina said.

"I went back to the hole a few weeks later for failure to lock down."

"You dint' tell me bout that," she said.

"It wasn't a big deal, the only reason I went to the hole cause a white boy got stabbed.

"Uh! Stabbed, what… why the fuck you dint tell me?"

"I don't wanna talk bout it."

"What the fuck you mean, you don't wanna talk bout it?" Sabrina's voice rose to a level where visitors looked over at their table.

Feeling a bit embarrassed, Possible dismissed the subject. "We'll talk bout it later, baby."

"You fuckin right we'll talk bout it."

"Lower your voice!" Possible said.

"You dint have nothing to do wit that, right?" Sabrina asked in a softer tone.

"No, baby."

"Maddy told me how it is in here wit all the politics and segregation stuff."

Possible looked at Maddy with a *Why?* expression.

"I told her how it used to be, when Charlie first came to prison. I told her a lot has changed from years ago when Charlie was locked up," Maddy explained, trying to justify telling Sabrina.

"How's my guy doing out there?" Possible asked.

"He's doin. Shit ain't been the same, of course, his right-hand man's gone, he don't trust anybody to do anything, so he's all over the place."

"What's up wit Shawn and Delvon?"

"They're Shawn and Delvon. you know, once you left, and Benny died, they haven't been too eager to be involved with the family business. Charlie tryna hire new people, but the market is changing. I told him he should look into selling the business."

Possible could feel his heart stop at the sound of selling the family business.

"No way!" That's one thing that can't ever happen." Possible said as he stared intensely into Maddy's eyes. "We've put too much into the business and lost too much; we have to figure it out."

"Well, we have to figure it out fast cause I'm pregnant, and Charlie will never tell you but we're struggling. Between BJ's sickle cell treatment and GG's frequent trips to the doctors, there's more going out than is comin in," Maddy said.

Possible's stomach began to knot up at the thought of his family struggling while he watched helplessly from prison. He'd never stopped to consider the effects his imprisonment had on Charlie and the family business.

"I even went back to workin at the club to help out," Sabrina added, not knowing how Possible might respond.

Maddy began, "I'm just saying we need to find a different market—"

"Fuck that! We *are* the market!" Possible said. "What Factor and Tommy doin?" Tommy and Factor were their two biggest investors and primary clientele.

"After that whole incident wit the Russians killin Benny, they're afraid of war breakin out, so they haven't been comin through. Charlie supposed to meet Tommy today and figure out some new distribution deal," Maddy said.

Possible sat in deep thought about why he hadn't told the truth about Benny's death. Maybe out of fear that Tommy and Factor would pull out completely, or of unwanted questions from the family. Whichever, it was affecting the bottom line. It seemed the truth would have been much easier to explain, and Tommy and Factor wouldn't be so paranoid about a war starting.

Maddy broke Possible's train of thought. "Ima go and get cards and dominos."

"Damn, baby, why dint you tell me all this was goin on?" Possible asked Sabrina.

"I dint wanna stress you or worry you. We can figure it out. You have enough to worry bout bein in here."

"That don't matter. I'm in prison, I'm not dead. I can contribute. What's goin on wit GG?"

"She good. She just gettin older, so when she gets sick it takes a different toll on her body."

"How many times she been to the hospital?"

"I lost count, but she's good, she just worried bout you and Charlie a lot."

"Ima start callin her more."

"That would help a lot," Sabrina replied.

"Baby, don't worry, everythin gonna be fine," Sabrina assured Possible, squeezing his hand.

"I should be tellin *you* that," Possible said.

"You do, just in other ways." Sabrina smiled and kissed his hand.

"I gotta pee," Sabrina said. She stood up. "Where the bathrooms?"

"Right by them double doors," Maddy said as she sat down with a deck of cards and a box of dominos.

"My bad, Maddy. I dint know it was this serious," Possible said. "I promise we gonna work it out, even if we have to sell as a last resort."

Possible knew he would die before selling the family business, but he understood what Maddy needed to hear for comfort and support.

"Thanks, Possible. You don't know how much Charlie misses you." Maddy's eyes began to fill with tears. "He hasn't been the same. He's distanced himself from me. He says the Russians killin Benny is his fault, and you bein here is his fault. He blames himself for everything and takes it out on me. I haven't even told him I'm pregnant."

Possible picked up a napkin to dab Maddy's face.

"I don't even know how to tell him."

It's all right, I'll tell him."

"Good God, no! Then he'll know I told you how bad everything is."

As Sabrina returned from the bathroom, she began to rub Maddy's back.

"I'm ruining you guys' visit bein hella hormonal," Maddy said.

"Bitch, please. We in this together," Sabrina assured her.

Possible grabbed the dominoes and began to wash, or shuffle, by sliding them around the tabletop in a circular motion. "Who's keepin score? Sabrina, you like to cheat. I don't know bout you keepin it," he teased.

"If Ima cheat, Ima cheat for you," Sabrina said with a sly grin.

Maddy said, "I'll keep it. Between the two of you, I don't know who'll cheat for who," she joked, grabbing the pen and paper from Sabrina.

As they began to play, Possible couldn't help but think about what he might do to help Charlie, to help the family. He'd thought riding the beef would help, but he wasn't so sure anymore. His heart was heavy. GG wasn't his biological grandma, but she'd never shown him that, and BJ wasn't his biological nephew, but BJ had told him that out of his three uncles—Possible, Delvon, and Shawn—Possible was his favorite. This was the only family Possible knew. Yeah, he had blood relatives, but he barely knew them. This was Possible's family, and he would die before he just sat back and watched them struggle financially, emotionally, physically, whatever. Struggle was unacceptable as long as he was around. As Possible laid down the dominos without any strategy, Dam'on walked past his table, catching Possible's attention, and a plan began to form in his head.

"Games and trash up," the visiting officer announced. "Bathrooms are closed. Five minutes till visits are over!"

"Ugh!" that went by quick," Sabrina said with a frown.

"I told you, girl, it's over before you know it," Maddy replied. "Ima put the games and trash up," she said, leaving to give Sabrina and Possible the last few minutes alone.

"Love you, Maddy," Possible said. "I appreciate you comin. Don't worry, we gonna figure everythin out. You just make sure you take care of my new nephew, or niece."

"I sure hope it's a girl, cause I'm done after this," Maddy said. She gave Possible a good-bye hug, then walked away.

"I might be able to put a couple things together," Possible said to Sabrina, "but Ima need your help."

"You know I got you, baby, whatever you need."

"Aight. Ima call—

"Visiting is over! Visitors to the door!"

"Ima call in a couple days," Possible said.

Sabrina stood to give him a long passionate kiss.

"Visitors to the door now! Visiting is over!"

"Aight, baby. Make sure you check your emails!" Sabrina said, then walked to the door and exited the visiting room.

"Bye, possible!" Maddy yelled, grabbing her ID from the guard.

"Aight, talk to y'all soon," Possible said.

"Tell Charlie Ima email!" Possible yelled as the door behind Maddy and Sabrina closed. Possible now knew exactly what to do for help.

Chapter 8

You're Forever in My Favor

"Did you have a good visit?" Dam'on asked.

After visiting time was over, the inmates waited to get strip-searched. Possible could never get used to standing buck naked and spreading his butt cheeks for another man, but this was how it had to be after every visit. On the way back to the unit, Possible meant to pick Dam'on's brain for advice—after all, Dam'on had said that if Possible ever wanted to pop it, to just let him know.

"This the worst part," Possible said, to grab Dam'on's attention.

"What's that?" Dam'on asked.

"The walk back to reality."

"That depends on your perception of reality. It could be the best part, a nice peaceful walk back, gives you the perfect opportunity to reflect on what just occurred. You were with people who know and care bout you; none of the people inside these walls can care bout you like the people you just left. For seven or eight hours you were on vacation, not worried bout anything guys in the unit are worried bout. You dint have to lift a finger the whole time. I saw you tonguin your girl. Felt good, right?"

"Right," Possible replied with a smile.

"See, make that your reality and your perception will make this the best part. There's guys will do a life sentence and never get to experience what you just experienced."

By then they had reached the unit and had to split to their respective pods.

"Aight, Dam'on," Possible said. He shook Dam'on's hand as they parted ways.

"We got yard tomorrow night. Come fuck wit me," Dam'on replied.

Possible walked into the unit with a different type of aura. He was smiling from ear to ear.

"Okay, I see you let me know it then, I ain't even gotta ask," Matt yelled from the other end of the dayroom as he swept the floor, part of his janitorial job. "We got dayroom in ten minutes," he added.

"I'll be out!" Possible shot back, walking.

"Bro, we got to talk!" Sweaty said.

"What happen?" Possible asked.

"While you was gettin ready for your visit you dropped a stick on the floor."

"Who found it?"

"I found it."

"Aight, we good then."

"Naw, my nigga, we not good. That coulda been all bad. What if we had yard and they did a security check? We'd be cooked," Sweaty said.

"You're not cooked, *I'm* cooked," Possible said.

"My nigga, you ain't in here by yourself. You think if they found somethin in here they gonna try and guess whose it is? Naw, we both go down."

"I wouldn't let you go down for my shit."

"It ain't bout that, Possible. You missin the point."

"I must be. Shit, I just came from a good visit and it's hella negative comin into the cell."

"Wouldn't *be* no more visits they woulda found that stick," Sweaty snapped back.

That was when it hit Possible that if he didn't take his time and pay attention to detail, he would jeopardize his situation and his cellmate's over something that could've been prevented by just being a bit more aware.

"You right. My bad."

"It's coo now. How was the visit?"

"Man, emotional, bomb, fun, overall it was poppin. Baby was lookin good, got to touch on some ass and kiss on some lips."

"That's how that goes," Sweaty said, smiling.

"Roll up."

"Roll up what?" asked Sweaty.

"You blew the stick?"

"Think of it as CO Peters found it, you won't be so mad," Sweaty replied.

"That's coo."

"Naw, I'm bout to get on at dayroom. We comin out right now," Sweaty announced, putting on his sweats and shoes. The cell doors began to open for dayroom. Sweaty and possible walked to the dayroom as inmates rushed to the phones and Jpay.

"Who's last for the Jpay?" yelled Possible.

"Me!"

"I'm after you," Possible said.

"Ay, boy, you shinin today," Matt joked about Possible's strut into the unit.

"Yeah, I had a good one, got to touch on some titties," Possible replied.

"You wasn't feelin no pussy though?" Sweaty teased.

"It's the first visit. Baby steps. We'll get there."

"Shit, I be all up in my girl pussy," Sweaty bragged.

"We getting' a table started or what?" Possible asked with a cold stare at Matt.

"I don't know what you muggin me for. I'm bout to watch the game. Lebron playin.'"

"Lebron!" Sweaty said with disgust.

"Thas right, Lebron mothafuckin James." Matt yelled as he walked into his cell.

"Ay, Possible, Jpay up!" an inmate yelled to tell Possible it was his turn.

"Here I come!" Possible made his way to the Jpay kiosk and logged in with his memorized password. The screen read 25 NEW MESSAGES. *Damn,* he thought, *they wasn't lyin bout the emails.*

"Who's after you?" one of the inmates asked.

"You," Possible answered. He sat and read his messages from Charlie, Sabrina, Maddy, Delvon, and a few people he didn't even recognize. He thought about calling Charlie, but decided not, considering how little time remained for dayroom.

"We bout to be on!" Sweaty announced with a grin as he walked by.

"Ay, we need to talk," Possible shot back.

"We can talk in the cell."

Through the dayroom intercom, CO Peters yelled, "Five minutes left for dayroom!"

"Yep, I'm outta here," Possible said to Sweaty.

"Here I come. Get some ice," Sweaty said.

Possible grabbed the ice pitcher as the cell door opened. "Jenkins!"

"Yeah!"

"Go see Officer Peters; he's got property for you!" CO Peters yelled through the cell intercom.

"Yep!"

Coming out of the cell on his way to pick up his property, Possible handed Sweaty the pitcher.

"Mr. Jenkins, I got some property for you. What's your DOC number?"

"J34126"

"All right, here's this." CO Peters handed Possible a list of the items he'd ordered. "Make sure everything on that list is in that bag. I'm assuming you already have a TV in the cell, right?"

"Yep," Possible answered.

"This will stay back here. If everything is there, sign and date here." As Possible went through the list, Peters studied him.

"Ay, you know a few weeks ago, the whole stabbing incident, I didn't wanna wrap you up like that."

Possible listened, but went on checking off the items on the list.

"I know shit goes on around here. I wasn't tryna single you out; you never gave me any problems."

At that point Possible looked up and made eye contact.

"I just wanted to make sure we're good—it wasn't personal," Peters said.

"Is it ever personal?" Possible asked.

"You'd be surprised at how vindictive some of these guards can get. I'll be honest, sometimes it does become personal."

Possible didn't know how to respond, so he just signed the paper and handed it to Peters.

"You're a good kid, Jenkins. Stay that way."

Possible gave Peters a half smile and took his new possessions back to his cell. It felt like today was his birthday—visit, new stuff—he couldn't be happier.

"Man, it must be your birthday!" Matt yelled out of the cell as he watched Possible carry his belongings to the cell.

"In the morning, my nigga. Have a good night!" Matt shouted.

"You know I will! You too!" The cell door slid open.

" Okay, I see you. Here, lemme grab somethin," Sweaty said, taking one of the three big brown bags from Possible. "You ordered everythin in one whomp?"

"Yeah."

"Visit, property, smoke on the next walk—feel like it's a nigga's birthday in this mothafucka. It goin down tonight!" Sweaty said, preparing the lighter. Possible began to arrange his property. He put all the everyday usables—hot pot, ice pitcher, fan, lamp, clippers—on his empty side of the shelf.

"Ooh, those the new Nikes?" Sweaty asked with excitement, inspecting the brand-new shoes.

"Now the cell looks complete," Possible said, smiling. Two guards walked by and that gave Sweaty the signal to get ready.

"Here, we facin one each tonight," Sweaty said, handing Possible a stick that looked like it'd been run over and put back together.

"Damn, my nigga, what happened to this?" Possible asked.

"Mines look like that too; my hands were sweaty.

"Don't try to bypass that last part. What you mean, your hands were sweaty?"

"That's why they call me Sweaty. I have a sweat condition, my palms and feet sweat a lot."

It all started to make sense: the sweaty socks, the barefoot prints on the cell floor, the tiny puddles.

"Mothafuckin Sweaty!" Possible teased.

"Whatever! You ready to blow?" Sweaty sparked his stick, then Possible's.

"Ooh, shit!" Possible began to cough harder than ever before. It felt like he was gonna cough up a lung. "Damn, this shit is fire!" he said, struggling to breathe.

"You got veins poppin out your forehead and shit," Sweaty said, pointing, laughing, and choking at the same time.

"That's okay," Possible replied, regaining his composure.

"How much did you get, if we're blowin sticks to the face."

"Don't worry bout where it came from, worry bout where it's goin, ain't that what you told me?" Sweaty mocked.

"Aight, I see," said Possible.

"Naw, I got a cap."

"What's a cap? How much can you make off that?" Possible asked, inhaling another cloud of smoke.

"Aight, aight, sit down here." Sweaty pulled out the cap of marijuana. Look, this is a cap. It's called a cap cause it supposed to be a ChapStick capful, which supposedly equals a gram," he explained. Sweaty set the ChapStick cap on the desk between them.

"This is your scale, so to speak. A full one of these is a hundred bucks. You get anywhere from seven to eight sticks out of a cap.

"How you supposed to make money off that?"

"Well, you don't. You buy caps to blow and to maybe get commissary stuff like hygiene and food."

"Fuck hygiene! How do you make money?"

"Well, you gotta buy enough quantity to be able to sell caps or more."

"We need to figure out how to get a quarter or a half. Shit, maybe even zips—ounces."

"You already know where to get that," Sweaty said, smiling as he threw away his roach.

"I know," Possible replied, tossing his own roach. "But I don't know how to ask. What—'Ay, Dam'on, lemme get a zip?'"

"Yep, just like that," Sweaty said.

"Yeah, right."

"Look, we got yard tomorrow night. Ima pop it wit him."

"He expects me, cause we was talkin on the way back from visits."

"You dint ask him then?"

"Naw. Fresh from the visit, I dint wanna come off as desperate."

"We need to sit down and put a plan together. We can't just get the shit and have a zip sittin in the cell," Sweaty said.

"I know, cause it's bout the bread. My people hurtin right now."

"Oh, it was one of *those* visits."

"What you mean one of those visits?" Possible asked, irritated.

"You know your people tell you bout what's goin on wit family and bills and you feel helpless cause you in prison, so you want to figure it out."

"You make it sound negative. Is that a problem?" Possible asked, his tone sarcastic.

"Not at all, just hard to cure problems if you don't know the diagnostics."

"What?"

"To identify the problem, you gotta know the symptoms."

"A smart dumb nigga. What was that supposed to explain?" Possible asked.

"Look, the what, how, and who needs to be worked out. How much we gettin?"

"A zip," Possible said.

"And who's gonna buy it—oh, and when are we gettin rid of it?"

"So we already got two out of four figured out, the who and how much. That's fifty percent. I'm sure we can figure out the rest. Look, my nigga, I know it's bad, but there's no other option," Possible said.

"I'm just sayin it's a whole different ballgame bustin moves for street money," Sweaty said. "Administration gets ahold a you and it's hard time."

"What's administration?"

"It's like the feds of the penitentiary. They over everybody, they do what they wanna do, and they not stupid."

"I thought you said Dam'on got it sold up?"

"Yeah, and what you think, they don't fuck wit him? Ask him. I'm sure he'll be happy to let you know how administration plays."

"I feel you, but I'm doing this regardless. It'd be a lot easier if I had your help."

"You're serious."

"As a heart attack," Possible said.

"Okay. Tomorrow Ima holla at Dam'on, but I can't guarantee nothin. We got a lot to do first. We gotta put together a team, get organized, and figure out the other half of the diagnostics."

"Look, I'm a solid nigga, bro. You help me put this together and I'll bring you in on our family business," Possible said.

"Family business? If you got a family business, what the hell we plottin this shit for?"

"That's the problem: the family business is goin under right now, and I need to give it CPR to bring it back to life."

Sweaty understood now what was at stake and how serious Possible was. He realized what type of commitment was needed, and how much it meant to Possible.

Sweaty took a deep breath and said, "I got you, my nigga," agreeing to whatever it would take.

"You forever in my favor," Possible replied. "I *am* my brother's keeper."

"I am my brother's keeper," Sweaty repeated.

"Aight, in the mornin then. It's hella late."

"In the mornin."

As they called it a night, Possible felt sure and confident, ready to embark on a new journey. For Sweaty it was different, he was all too familiar with this kind of journey, one that came with all types of twists and turns that could lead you somewhere you never wanna be. Sweaty closed his eyes and prayed that this journey would be brief.

Chapter 9

The Person You Thought You Knew, You Never Knew

The next morning, Possible, Sweaty, and Matt sat at the breakfast table, brainstorming on the more lucrative pathway.

"I'm tellin you," Matt said, "we need to sell to Dam'on."

"I hear you," Possible said, "but you think Dam'on gonna be coo wit that? And besides, how we gonna go from not even havin a plug to *bein* the plug?"

"That's why we need to figure a way to find out what Dam'on's prices are, and beat them," said Sweaty.

"No, stupid, I'm talkin bout undercuttin Dam'on's plug so *we* become his plug, we beat whoever he picks up from," said Matt.

"That ain't what you said," Sweaty shot back.

"You always—"

"Ay! Ay! "Possible snapped, causing guards and inmates to stare. "Look, we gonna find out Dam'on's prices first, then look for a plug to beat his prices," Possible explained in a forceful tone. "In the meantime we keep everythin on the down-low. We don't want people tryna figure out what we got goin on."

"What we need to do is find a way to get it ourselves. That way no one can beat our prices, Matt said.

"You say that like that's the easy part," Sweaty said.

"That's not what I said," Matt retorted.

"Look, I need you two to be coo. This ain't no sports debate, my nigga, we gotta be on point, less attention as possible, so all the arguin gotta stop. I'm serious. My family is hurtin, and all this is ridin on whether we make this work," Possible said.

Matt had never seen Possible so demanding and so passionate, and he knew this was a big deal. "I got you," he said.

"You already know wit me," added Sweaty.

"Aight then, we all on the same page," Possible said.

The three rose from the breakfast table with three different ideas and agendas, but all had the same motive. Matt and Sweaty understood Possible's situation, but they had their own situations as well, so this was beneficial for all three. Back in the unit, it was afternoon dayroom, and there was a different vibe in the unit. CO Peters and CO Peters could sense the change: no poker table, no crowd of people watching poker being played, but long lines for the phone and Jpay.

"What's good my nigga?" Possible asked Charlie over the phone.

Shit, waitin on you to hit me."

"Did you get my emails?" Possible asked.

"Yeah, I shot one back," Charlie said. "How was your visit?"

"Man, it was the [shitnitite], ate real good, got to touch on Sabrina."

"All the shit and stuffses?" asked Charlie.

"All the shit and stuffses," Possible replied.

"They said they goin back up there soon," Charlie said. "Make sure you keep in touch so you'll know when they comin."

"Ay, bro, lemme ask you somethin," Possible said.

"Yeah?"

"What's goin on wit Factor and Tommy?"

"What you mean, what's goin on?"

"Why they trippin bout the Russians?"

Charlie knew what Possible was asking, but didn't want to talk about it over the phone.

"Naw, there was a misunderstandin when everythin first happened, but everythins good now. I actually met wit Tommy the other day. We just put together a new distribution deal stretchin to Eastern Washington, so shit bout to get better," Charlie said.

"Aight, but you know if you need help wit somethin or you just need to talk, I can help, right?" Possible wanted to assure Charlie that he was still his right-hand man.

"My nigga, you already know," Charlie said. "But you're not in the position right now, and I don't think it's a good idea to be playin around in there." This was the best way Charlie could explain that he didn't want Possible hustling in prison. "I told you, stay out the way, we good."

"You have sixty seconds remaining," the automated voice said.

"Aight, bro. There's a few ideas Ima have Sabrina run by you."

"You have thirty seconds remaining."

"Aight, Peety. Love you, bro. Keep your head up," said Charlie just before the phone call was cut off.

New distribution deal, thought Possible. Maybe things weren't that bad after all, and the ladies were just overreacting. Possible knew how Sabrina could get, but he also knew that Maddy wouldn't get all emotional and worried over nothing. Possible would continue with his agenda, and if Charlie made everything happen, then Possible's idea would be a bonus for the family business.

"Possible, let me holla at you," Matt said.

"What's good?"

"Look, I just got off the phone wit my people, and we can put the shit together in a few days," Matt said.

"Yep, but we gotta find a way in," Possible replied.

"I thought we was gonna fuck wit Dam'on. I know *he* know a way in."

"Yeah, but we have to make it right enough for him to want to fuck wit us," said Possible.

"Look, I'll just holla at him tonight at yard."

"Naw, Sweaty already got that part, plus Dam'on told me he fucks wit Sweaty, he said just don't let him drive, whatever that means."

"Exactly what you're lettin him do, be in charge of shit. Sweaty's a coo guy, but you got him in the wrong spot."

"Let me holla at Dam'on. I'll work it out wit Sweaty and we'll go from there."

"Make sure Sweaty coo wit that. Look, my nigga, we got to put our egos aside and come together for a bigger purpose," Possible said.

"You think you the only one that need this? My family hurtin too. I got six kids and seven baby mamas."

Possible looked confused. " How you got six kids but seven baby mamas?"

"Cause the bitch I'm wit now, her kid ain't mines. I take care of her and the kid like it's mines, so you ain't the only one tryna make shit happen."

Possible felt bad about all the time he'd been fucking with Matt he'd never even known—being down for nineteen years must get stressful.

"I got you. I'll let Sweaty know after we lock down."

"Dam'on knows who's who, If we wanna be taken seriously let me talk to him," said Matt.

"Aight, that's the plan. Me and Sweaty will put together the other shit," Posible assured Matt.

CO Peters voice boomed through the dayroom intercom:. "Five minutes till dayroom is closed, last call for ice. Big yard's tonight, so get ice now."

"Aight, my nigga, at big yard."

"Yep, at big yard." Matt shook Possible's hand and went into his cell. Possible hoped Sweaty could put his ego to the side and not feel a certain way about Matt talking to Dam'on instead of him. Everything Matt said made perfect sense; Possible just had to get Sweaty to see it the same way.

Chapter 10

Underplay for the Overplay

Possible celled in and found Sweaty already there, sitting on the bottom bunk preparing his conversation with Dam'on while rolling a stick.

"Ay, I'm just gonna let Dam'on know we hungry. We tryna get on, but not wit no small shit," Sweaty said.

"You sure you okay to roll that?" asked Possible, seeing Sweaty's hands perspiring with heat.

"Here, you twist." Sweaty switched places with Possible.

"You feel me?" Sweaty said, pacing back and forth. "Ain't no sense tryna beat 'round the bush bout what we tryna do."

"Bout that, I think if Matt holla at him, you know wit Matt bein down round the same amount of time he'll be able to connect more wit Dam'on."

Sweaty stopped pacing and just stared at Possible.

Over the intercom, the booth officer yelled," Standing count! You must be standing up or sitting on your bunk!"

"Who decided that?" Sweaty asked.

"That's irrelevant. This ain't bout egos or swagger. We need to figure who's best to do what, and we come together as one," Possible said sternly.

"I ain't trippin bout none of that. We just need to make sure *we* all on the same page when it comes to the finances," Sweaty replied.

"What, you don't trust Matt?"

"I don't trust my own mom!" Sweaty snapped.

There was an awkward silence, which allowed Possible to hear the unit door close.

"Don't trip. I feel you, we gonna make sure shit done right," Possible assured Sweaty while sparking the stick.

"I'm not sayin Matt on some funny, I'm just sayin I don't *know* if he on some funny."

"Naw, Matt seems like a straight shooter. I got a good sense bout 'im," Possible said, passing the stick.

"I know you do, but I been round a li'l bit and I know that when bread gets involved, other traits come out—the person you thought you knew, you never knew," Sweaty shot back.

"Is it me, or every time we blow, you sound all profound and shit," Possible joked, grabbing the stick.

"You know what they say bout bud?"

"Naw, what they say?" Possible asked, inhaling a cloud of smoke.

"Bud enlightens you, it opens up your third eye."

"Boof, ha-ha-ha-ha. This nigga said bud opens your third eye," Possible said, trying to regain his composure from laughing so hard.

"Oh, you, think I'm jokin? I made this shit up? You never heard people refer to their third eye?" Sweaty asked.

"No, nigga!"

"It's called the pineal gland, if you wanna get technical."

The booth-officer announced, "Count cleared. H-unit, prepare for mainline! H-unit, mainline!"

"What's for dinner?" Possible asked.

"Check the menu!" Sweaty snaps.

"Ugh! Spaghetti," Possible said with a disgusted look. "I'm not goin."

"How bout goin over the plan before yard tonight?" Sweaty asked.

"We already got the plan. Anything new we can discuss it on the way to yard."

"You got high and got lazy!" said Sweaty.

"I'm bout to put one of these meat sticks in the hot pot, put some mayonnaise, barbeque sauce, and ranch on bread, open these Doritos wit some Hawaiian Purple Smash drink and be good.

"Shit, the way you put that together, make me one too," demanded Sweaty.

"You eatin spaghetti," Possible teased.

"I'm bout to holla at Matt, make sure we on the same page." No ego shit," Possible urged.

"Pod 2, mainline! Pod 2, mainline!"

"I got you, bro," Sweaty said with a smirk as he left the cell.

With his cellie gone for at least twenty minutes, Possible had some time to himself. He had no intentions of fixing a meat stick with barbeque sauce, mayonnaise, and all that other shit. It sounded good, but that was to throw his cellie a curveball. Possible had been thinking about Sabrina and her big titties and fat ass. Possible pulled out some of the sexy pics she had sent including some booty shorts pics he'd just downloaded on his player, and grabbed a bottle of lotion. He could feel the blood flowing to his penis. This sight of Sabrina's ass alone was enough to make him come, but he wanted to enjoy this. He swiped right on his tablet with his left hand, and used his right hand to jerk off. Pic after pic after pic he could feel himself getting ready to climax. Grabbing one of the Polaroids with his left hand, visualizing his penis in Sabrina's mouth, he could no longer hold back and ejaculated into a towel. As he began to put the photos away, staring at them intensely, he felt another urge shoot through him. Figuring he had enough time, he starts again, this time focusing only on the photos.

With a sudden *click!* the door popped open. Frantically, Possible jumped up to find his towel. He wiped himself off and looked to see Sweaty coming up the stairs in conversation with Matt.

"Damn!" As Possible rushes to put the photos away, he heard Matt calling him.

"Possible, boy, you missed it."

The door swung open. "What's good, my nigga?" Sweaty asked, sensing something wrong.

"Shit, just uh, um, bout to cook," Possible said, breathing heavily.

Matt stood in the doorway and stared Possible up and down, inspecting the scene while Sweaty did the same from inside the cell. He spotted the bottle of lotion and Sabrina's ass blown up big on the tablet.

"Ha-ha-ha-ha, this nigga in here bein nasty!" Sweaty said, holding up the tablet.

"Let me see!" Matt asked, reaching for the tablet.

Before Sweaty could hand it to Matt, Possible snatched it back. "I was *tryna* be nasty, but clearly you dint get the hint," he said.

"You shoulda said that instead of makin up some fake-ass meal you was gonna make," Sweaty said.

"I thought what's understood don't have to be said."

"Yeah, yeah. Anyway, we got the game plan," Sweaty said.

Through the intercom, the booth officer ordered Matt: "Richardson—find your cell!"

"Aight, bro, bring him up to speed. Ima see y'all at yard," Matt said, closing their cell door as he walked off.

"So, we got a understandin bout the whole convo wit Damon," Sweaty said.

"Oh, yeah? What that?" Possible asked.

"Matt just gonna let him know we tryna get on wit big shit, and dependin on how he responds we go from there!"

"What do you mean, 'how he responds'?"

"Well, if he can fill the order or not. It's like, if he can, then you ask a question hopin to catch somethin else. We ask how much, then the price he gives us, we know what we gotta beat."

"And if we can't?"

Sweaty gave a cheesy grin. "Then we ask how we can help him help us get it," Sweaty said.

"Sounds like a solid plan," Possible said.

"The only thing is, we need to make sure our paper right, if he puts us on the spot and asks if we ready right now," Sweaty replied.

"I thought you stay ready so you don't have to get ready—oh, that's only wit wakin up in the mornin," Possible teased.

"Shit, I got my half."

"Aight then, what's the problem?" Possible asked.

"Matt said he ain't on right now."

Possible shrugged. "I got 'im. We'll figure out the rest later."

"Well, we good then, my nigga. We bout to be on!" said Sweaty.

Seeing how excited Sweaty was, Possible couldn't help but smile. Possible was used to being on; this was what he'd done his entire life, just not in prison.

"All them bitches that left a nigga for broke and dead, I'm bout to stunt on them bitches," Sweaty said. "I'm bout to show 'em, 'I bet your nigga ain't on like this! Yeah, I'm booked, but look at this! Ha-ha-ha!"

"Calm down! I told you this ain't bout that," Possible said.

"Yeah, but you can't tell me what to do wit my share," Sweaty replied.

"You right, but Ima tell you like Charlie told me: We do this cause we have to, not cause we want to. When our paper right, then we do what we want to."

"Oh, yeah, I like that. Let's roll up before yard. Who's Charlie?

As Possible and Sweaty sat smoking, laughing and joking about Sweaty's sweat condition, the booth officer called yard: "Big yard, Pod 2!" he yelled.

"Oh shit, my nigga, it's still hella smoky," Possible said.

"Don't get all paranoid now—you wasn't paranoid when you dropped that stick," Sweaty teased, putting on his shoes and jacket.

"So we back to that?" Possible asked, popping the cell door. The two walked out onto the tier.

"Man, it sho must be nice!" Matt said, referring to the two being high.

"Don't even trip, I got you right here," Sweaty said, handing Matt a stick.

"That's two in one. I know you in the single-man cell, so you don't have to share," Sweaty said.

"I sho 'preciate it."

"It's wrapped good, too," Sweaty added.

Matt waited till they'd walked past the booth and onto the breezeway before hiding the stick in his mouth in order to get through the pat search.

"Sweaty gave me the game plan. I like it," Possible told Matt.

"Did he tell you bout the bread?" Matt asked.

"Don't even trip, we'll just work out the details later. As the three men walked up on the row of guards waiting to search them, Possible noticed Ms. Hunter and instantly began to count how many inmates were in line and how many guards, so he could get pat searched by her. He had to let Sweaty pass, and saw Sweaty smirk.

"How you doin, Ms. Hunter?"

"Not bad. How about yourself?"

"Oh, you know, another day in paradise."

"Paradise, huh?"

After the pat search, Possible turned to look her in the eyes and flashed a smile. To his surprise, CO Hunter smiled back.

"Have a good yard," Hunter shouted as the three men entered the yard.

"Another day in paradise?" Sweaty mocked. "Oh, yeah. You shootin alright," he added.

"You seen all them guards, listenin," Possible snapped.

Where Dam'on?" Sweaty asked impatiently.

"Chill. We out here for the next hour and some," Possible said.

"He comin right out through the gate," said Sweaty.

Dam'on entered the yard, met up with the Burgundy B's, greeted them with their handshake, and then walked toward Possible, Sweaty, and Matt.

"Here he comes right now," Sweaty whispered

"I can see him coming," Matt whispered back.

"Chill!" Possible said.

"Why you niggas looking like the three stooges and shit?" Dam'on asked.

"Ay, lemme bend a lap wit you?" Matt asked, stepping out the group.

"You wanna bend a lap wit me?" Dam'on replied sarcastically, and eyed the other two suspiciously as Matt started to lead the way.

"He knows we up to somethin," Sweaty said.

"Yeah, you niggas all huddled up and lookin all nervous," Possible snapped.

"It's all good, they poppin it right now," Sweaty replied.

"What's good?" Zay and I Like it Here walked up and greeted Sweaty and Possible.

"What's up, Possible? Sweaty ain't put you on yet?" Zay asked in reference to joining the City G's.

"I'm already on!" Possible responded.

"Calm down, tiger. I'm just fuckin wit you," Zay said. I Like It Here cracked a smile.

"What y'all got goin on?" Sweaty asked.

"Shit, tryna see what's good wit some smoke. J-money tole us you got pack," Zay said.

"Damn nigga talk too much. How that nigga know?" asked Sweaty. "It don't even matter. I brought you somethin, anyway, wanted it to be a surprise," Sweaty said, handing Zay two pieces of plastic.

"Good lookin!" I Like it Here said.

"You already know, I'm on, y'all on." Sweaty said, giving their special handshake.

Possible sat back and watched how Sweaty treated Zay and I Like It Here. Even if they didn't ask, Sweaty was still going to put them on.

"It's time to get organized. We got a plan in motion, so be ready," Sweaty said.

Zay and I Like It Here knew exactly what Sweaty was saying without his saying it.

"Just say the word, we here." Zay replied.

"Ay, I almos forgot, them niggas in Pod 1 trippin. I guess one of the City niggas got into it wit one of the Royal C's over some poker or somethin," Zay said.

"Who from the City?'

"I don't know, some nigga name Boomby, Buggy,—"

"Bumby?" Sweaty asked

"Yeah, you know him?"

"Yeah, he from the Gardens," Sweaty said.

"I think I was in juvie wit 'im," I Like it Here said.

"What happen wit him and the Royal C nigga?" Sweaty asked.

Just then, Matt came back to the group and interrupted the conversation. "He wanna talk to you," Matt said to Possible.

"Me?"

"Yeah, you!"

"What did he say?"

"He said he wanna talk to you."

"All that time that's all y'all talked bout?"

"Yeah, he said he wanna talk to you."

I Like It Here and Zay were looking confusedly at Sweaty, and Sweaty was looking at Matt.

"Why you niggas actin suspicious?" asked Zay.

"Aight," Possible said, and walked off toward the Burgundy B's. Possible had tried to eavesdrop and find out what had happened with the City G and Royal C, but had walked out of earshot before Zay could explain.

Approaching the group, Possible asked, "What's good, Dam'on?"

"Ay, Possible, what's good? You met J-money and Li'l D. This is T, Shmoney, Mack, and JB. This is Possible, y'all."

"What's good!" the four replied.

"Let's bend, ay, homie? Ima be right back, don't go nowhere!" Dam'on said, looking at Shmoney.

"Aight," Shmoney said, frowning.

"So what you niggas got goin on?" Dam'on asked Possible as the two began to walk.

"What you mean?" Possible shot back nervously.

"Look, my nigga, I been knowin Matt for a minute, and he has never been in a position to get what he tryna get," Dam'on said.

"Aight, look, my nigga, my family is out there strugglin. I'm just tryna put together a few moves to help out."

"Let me tell you somethin bout me," Dam'on said. "You always get more out of me by bein a hunnid. If shit don't add up, then my attennas go up, and once they're up it's hard to get 'em back down."

"Naw, wasn't no funny shit. It's just I just met you, and I dint know how you'd react to me comin at you like that," Possible said.

"You got a lot to learn. When I introduced myself to you few weeks back, that's what I was doin, openin the door. I shot you two sticks and told you we can pop it anytime. If I was gonna react any type of way, by that introduction you know what type of response you'd get."

Possible smiled. "You right. My bad."

"Don't even trip. You just realizin what type of nigga you fuckin wit. When me and Matt was talkin, he was askin a bunch of questions bout prices, and I just told him Ima holla at you."

I guess Matt wasn't lyin, Possible thought.

"So, how much you tryna pick up?"

"How much you got?" Possible asked.

"Look, y'all got your bread right? You got clientele?" Dam'on asked.

"I mean, how hard can that be, find people in prison that get high?" Possible said.

"So, what? You gonna cop, then go round askin who wanna buy, and at the same time you're waitin for people to cop, you're blowin too?"

"I guess I dint see it from that perspective."

"Why don't we give you a test run. I got a joog in your pod who's good for two hundred a week. I'll put you on wit that and see what comes of it."

"No disrespect, but I don't wanna be pushin for anybody. I appreciate the opportunity, but I'm tryna do my own thing," Possible replied.

Dam'on stopped and stared. "I thought you was in this to help your family out. Did I miss somethin?"

"No, but I'm not tryna be responsible for anybody's work," Possible said.

"When I first met you, you said you get money," Dam'on said. "What type of money is that if you can't tell the difference between a front or a put-on? I'm not tryna have you responsible for anythin. I'm tryna turn your water on. You're responsible for how long it runs."

"I got my niggas, too. We goin fifty-fifty on everythin, so—

"Ima stop you there. I deal wit you and only you. This is business, not personal."

Possible felt exactly what Dam'on was saying. Charlie had taught him the same shit. "I feel you. So you only deal wit me," Possible agreed.

"So don't send no more niggas to me askin prices and shit. What Ima do is shoot a whole zinger to you in your bag on laundry day. In it will be the info and how to send the cake, the joog too," Dam'on said. "Also this prob'ly be the last time we talk like this. Niggas see you movin an talkin to me, they try to connect the dots. Next thing you know we dealin wit I'll-Kiteya."

"You mean Al-Qaeda, like the terrorist group?" Possible asked.

"Yeah, they might as well be terrorists, but it's I'll-Kiteya right out the unit," said Dam'on.

Possible couldn't help but chuckle.

Dam'on said, "We talk a couple more times to get our system of operation down till it works without us havin to do this."

Possible understood exactly what he meant—this was the language he spoke. "When will the first drop-off be?" he asked.

"The next laundry day. Never let anyone know the laundry is the source. Once the source is compromised, so is the operation, so make sure when you get the bag, you don't even let your cellie know or see you get the bag. I strongly advise that you never keep anything in the cell, ever. Be smart, pay attention to detail, know your environment, how shit move, what shift to do what on," Dam'on explained.

"Yep." Possible replied. He felt like a computer downloading all this data and internalizing it.

"I'm an understanding guy," Dam'on said. "So when it comes to bread, just be a hunnid wit me. I already told you bout the antennas, so let's make this a good thing. Who knows—one day you might rise to be the next kingpin."

"I'm just tryna get my family back right. I don't know nothin bout all that king shit," Possible replied.

Dam'on just smiled. He remembered when he'd first started. His father had gotten sick, and needed money for chemo treatment. That was ten years ago, and his father had been cancer-free for five years, and Dam'on was still moving like he had to pay for the treatment. *You're gonna be all right, Possible,* Dam'on thought. *You're gonna be all right.*

"On the next night yard, we'll meet up to go over everythin, just to make sure we on the same page," Dam'on said.

"I really mean it when I say I 'preciate this," Possible said.

"I know you do," said Dam'on.

They shook hands, then split, going their separate ways. As Possible walked up to Matt, he could see Sweaty having an intense conversation with a group of City G's.

"What's goin on over there?" Possible asked Matt.

"Uh, shit, somethin bout one of them niggas owin somethin or somebody somethin I don't know. Fuck all that! What Dam'on say?"

"We on!"

"How on?"

"Whatever we want. I'm bout to pick up in a few days," Possible said with a huge smile.

"How we splittin everythin."

"We gonna discuss all that over breakfast tomorrow, me, you, and Sweaty."

"We can do that at dayroom. You know random niggas be tryna sit at the table, noisy-ass niggas."

"Yep, that's even better. When do you think you'll have your part of the bread?" Possible asked.

"How much he chargin?"

"I don't know yet. He gonna shoot everythin at me in a few days."

"Aight. Shit, I should be ready in a few days then," Matt replied.

"Aight. I'm bout to see what's good wit these guys over here."

"I'm bout to use the phone," Matt shot back.

As Possible walked up to the group of City G's, he could tell this was a serious situation.

"Ay, my nigga, you in violation," Possible could hear Sweaty say to one of the men.

"What's good?" Possible asked.

"Hold up. Ay, Possible, we handlin City business here," Sweaty snapped. "You and me gonna talk when we get back to the cell."

"Ay, my bad," Possible said.

"You good, my nigga," Sweaty assured him, then returned his attention to the group. With Matt on the phone and Sweaty giving a lecture, Possible found himself alone in the yard, debating whether to use the phone. He decided to do a few pull-ups and dips instead.

"Ay, I'm next, homie!"

"My bad—where the end of the line at?" Possible asked.

"You after me," one of the Mexicans replied.

"One, two, three, what's your name homie?" The Mexican doing pull-ups asked.

"Possible!"

"Like two and a possible," the man teased.

Possible just smiled; he'd heard every joke to be heard regarding his name.

"Yeah, why not," Possible replied with a smile.

"I'm Joker."

"That's fittin," Possible replied. "Nice to meet you, homie."

"I got you, homes," Joker said, as he and his workout partner left.

Alone now, Possible was doing pull-ups and dips, and thinking about the strategy he'd just put into motion. He knew these two Mexicans were cool with Sweaty—that was the whole point of the pull-ups and dips—and of course he knew where to find smoke, but when Joker come back tomorrow to let Possible know where to go and how much to ask for and the price, Possible could gauge the market. A smokescreen. Charlie had taught him this: he called it the under play for the over play.

"Yard closed!" Line up on the fence, One minute on the phones! Yard in!

Chapter 11

I'm Just Adapting to My Environment, That's All

The next morning, as the two got ready for breakfast, Sweaty still had attitude from the previous night's yard situation.

"That shit still don't make sense to me," Possible said, brushing his teeth.

"It's only not makin sense cause the homie dint handle his business."

"Why don't he just chalk it up as a loss?" Possible asked.

"Naw. There's certain losses, comin from where I come from, that's unacceptable, and somebody tellin you he ain't gonna pay is one of 'em. That's automatic take-off," Sweaty said. "Now this homie Bumpy is in the middle and bout to get 'em up wit the nigga, and this nigga think he gonna get off, but that ain't how it's goin down, so if this nigga D-man don't take off on the nigga, then Bumpy gonna do it, and Zay gonna take off on D-man," Sweaty explained.

"All that shit sounds dumb over a couple bucks," Possible said, with an irritated attitude.

"Look, my nigga, I don't know how you do it where you from, but niggas from the City have a zero-tolerance policy for disrespect, especially blatant disrespect. You in the fuckin jungle wit gorillas and lions and shit; the moment you show any sign of weakness you lose your spot in the peckin order in this animal kingdom. You know what happens to gazelles in the jungle? Sweaty didn't wait for an answer. "They get eaten by all the big cats."

"I'preciate the *Big Cat Diary* lesson, but we gotta finish puttin this bread together," Possible said, putting on his shoes.

"That's what I'm sayin!" We tryna put shit together, lettin shit like this slide in this kinda business is no good," Sweaty said.

"Yeah, but this ain't no card game, either," Possible replied.

The booth officer announced: "Pod 2, prepare for mainline. IDs on, shirts tucked in. Pod 2, prepare for mainline."

"That's the point. You nip this type of shit in the bud at the lowest levels; that way, when it comes to the higher levels, a tone been set," Sweaty said, popping the cell door open to go eat.

"Well, when you put it that way, it make sense," Possible said, as he walked out behind Sweaty.

"This guy in here is [curbed,]" Sweaty announced to Possible as the two walked past Matt's cell.

"You not eatin?" Possible asked Matt, jerking the handle of his cell door.

"We gonna talk at dayroom!" Matt yelled, refusing to get up.

On the way to mainline, Sweaty noticed a lot of commotion in Pod 1.

"What's goin on over there?" Possible asked.

"I don't know, but that better be D-man handlin business," Sweaty said.

"They cuffin guys," Possible shot back.

As the two tried to leave the pod, movement was stopped, and through the windows, Sweaty could see it wasn't D-man.

"That's Bumpy and the nigga from the Royal C's," Sweaty said, thinking out loud.

"Mainline! Mainline!" Movement has resumed," the booth officer announced. The door to the pod popped open and the inmates headed to chow hall.

"Ay, homie, where D-man at?" Sweaty asked a Black inmate from Pod 1 as the two were passing.

"He bout to come out the chow hall," the man replied, slow-walking, hoping to see a fight.

"You gonna handle that like we just discussed?" Possible asked.

Sweaty gave no answer as the two hit the breezeway to the chow hall.

"Bro, not out here like this!" Possible snapped.

"I got you, my nigga!" Sweaty replied.

As the two entered the chow hall they were met with stares from every inmate—whites, APIs, Natives, Mexicans, and of course Blacks. The chow hall got so quiet you could hear a rat pissing on cotton. Sweaty spotted D-man in line waiting to tray up.

"D-man, mornin yard, homie!" Sweaty yelled across the room. Normal conversation broke out again as the inmates got back to everyday bullshit.

"Damn, that was intense, my nigga. You see them watchin you and shit?" Possible asked.

"I don't give a fuck bout none of that," Sweaty said as the two grabbed their breakfast trays and sat next to J-money, Li'l D, Zay, and I Like It Here.

"Here, Possible. We outta here," Li'l D said, offering Possible his seat.

"Aight, my niggas, y'all be coo," J-money said to the four as he and Li'l D left to tray up.

"Was that Bumpy and the nigga?" I Like It Here asked.

"Yeah," Sweaty said. "Why dint D-man go?"

"Man, this nigga was in here actin like he was goin to another joint or somethin," Zay said.

"All these long good-byes, and 'aight my niggas' and shit," I Like It Here added. "We told him to go handle that. I think he was stallin. We don't got yard today, and tomorrow Zay got visit, so Ima take care of it at mornin yard."

"Hopeful he bring his scary ass to yard, he know what time it is," Sweaty said.

Possible just sat in disbelief at how something so trivial as a $20 poker debt could turn into something so serious.

"I got ten bucks the nigga checks in," Zay said.

"Fuck that nigga!" Sweaty snapped.

"No takers!"

"I see that ten," Possible chimed in.

"Oh, okay, I ain't gotta worry bout gettin paid fuckin wit you," Zay told Possible, prompting a smile from I Like It Here.

"Bonds and Grant, time's up. Let's go," the chow hall CO demanded.

"Aight, y'all." Zay said, as the CO was telling him and I Like it Here to leave.

"Shit, we outta here too. You done eatin?" Sweaty asked Possible.

"Yep, let's dip."

All four picked up their trays and left the chow hall. On the breezeway Possible spotted Ms. Hunter.

"How you doin, Ms. Hunter?" Possible asked.

"Y'all staying out of trouble?" Ms. Hunter asked.

"On our best behavior!" mocked Sweaty.

"Damn, she thick," Zay said.

"Have a nice day!" Possible shouted as Ms. Hunter walked off.

"You too!" she replied.

"I'm tellin you, I'm wearin her down," Possible whispered.

"Nigga, please!" Sweaty shot back as they entered the unit.

"Ay, Possible, you comin to lunch?" asked Joker, exiting the unit with his workout partner.

"Yep."

"Aight, homie. What's up, Sweaty?"

"Joker!" shouted Sweaty. "What y'all got goin on?" he asked as Joker strolled away.

"Don't even trip, you already know," Possible replied. Entering the unit, the four split, going to their respective pods.

Later that day, Matt, Possible, and Sweaty were high as hell in the dayroom as they went over the finances and split of everything.

"So look, Dam'on ain't trippin. I'm bout to pick up in a few days. That's when I'll know the prices on everythin. I say just have $250 apiece on deck," Possible said.

"For the whole zinger?' Matt asked.

"Yeah, we gonna bust it down three ways, and make sure you got your part when it's time to reup, and we keep it moving like that," Possible said.

"How is he gonna get the zinger to you?" Sweaty asked.

"So we not fightin over joogs, let's just work together and get the whole thing off," Possible said, ignoring Sweaty's question.

"I *know* you heard me," Sweaty said.

"What?"

"My nigga, what's up wit the attitude?" Sweaty asked.

"Naw, I dint hear you," Possible said.

"How is he gonna get the zinger to you?" Sweaty repeated, louder.

"He don't want nobody to know," Possible said.

"You coulda just said that, stead of actin like you dint hear me," Matt snapped, irritated at Possible's not giving up the source.

"Look, my nigga, Ima tell you the real: he don't even wanna deal wit you guys. He said this on me and he's only dealin wit me, and I deal wit y'all. This ain't a group thing to him," Possible said.

"I respect that," Sweaty said.

"That's coo," Matt added.

"Coo. Then we all on the same page, let's get this bread," Possible said.

"So you just want baby to shoot your girl this bread now or what?" Sweaty asked.

"Yeah, so we don't have to scramble to get the bread together," Possible replied.

"Yup, Ima hop on the phone now and put that together," Sweaty said.

"I told you already, I'll have mines in a couple days," Matt said.

"Joker told me he can get two caps for $185. I told him I'm good, I found two for $150, Possible said.

"Oh, look at you takin my moves. It's all good, it's all goin to the same pot," said Sweaty.

"Also Dam'on shootin a joog he be fuckin wit in this pod," Possible told them.

"Shit, it sounds like we're ready to reup already," Matt said, grinning.

"That's how that goes," Sweaty said.

"I ain't tryna be sittin on shit and havin the cell hot," Possible said.

"Shit, if that mothafucka gonna be hot cause smoke comin from it, we ain't gonna have shit sittin nowhere!" Matt joked.

Sweaty and possible laughed as the three realized they were still high.

"I'm outta here, I'm bout to use the phone," Possible announced, walking away from the two.

"Yep, aight." Sweaty and Matt said in unison.

Possible walked to the phone feeling excited to talk to GG. He understood that he needed to call more often, and today he would start.

"Hello," GG said. "Boy you ought to be ashamed of yourself."

"What I done now GG?"

"You called and got that number and I ain't hear from you since. Charlie told me you don't call him either. What you doin in there?"

"GG, I'm in close custody. I don't come out like that, and it's hard to get to the phone when I can come out," Possible lied.

"Boy, don't sit up dere and lie like that. I know how it go, I used to be married to a man dat did five years. If you wanna call me bad enough you'll find a way to call yo grandma!"

It hurt Possible's feelings to hear how upset GG was by the fact he hadn't called.

"You right, GG. I—"

"I know I'm right," she interrupted.

"Ima make it a habit to start callin more, I promise."

"Aight, dats much betta. Don't lie to yo grandmama. I know you get caught up wit dem people in dere, but don't forget bout yo people out here. We love you and wanna hear from you."

"I know, GG. I'm gonna do better. You got my word on that."

"Make sure you start callin Charlie too. He feel like I feel. We worry when we don't hear from you."

"Yes, ma'am, How you been doin?" Possible asked.

"Uh, I'm doin much betta dan I was. I just got out the hospital three days ago. I had a sharp pain shoot through my back makin me not able to walk. Den I had a dizzy spell yesterday, but God is good, I'm feelin much better, walkin again, talkin to my baby.

This put a smile on Possible's face. It warmed his heart to hear GG call him her baby.

"I'm glad to hear you doin better. Ima make sure I pray for you."

"Yeah, baby, prayer's powerful. I wrote a song the other night before my dizzy spell made me stop. When I finish Ima sing it for you."

"Let me hear what you got!" Possible said, excited.

"Naw, naw, Ima wait till it's all done cause I'm still fixin it—and it assures me you gonna call back," said GG.

Possible could hear the smile in GG's voice when she said that.

"Aight, Ima hold you to that too, so when I call back in a few days, I don't wanna hear it's not ready yet."

"Boy, you know I ain't gonna say nothin I ain't gonna do."

"How's everybody doin?" Possible asked.

"Everybody's doin. It just ain't the same out here witout you, baby."

"You have sixty seconds remaining," the automated voice announced.

"I know, GG. I'll be home sooner than you know."

"I hope so. I was—"

The robot voice cut her off: *Thirty seconds remaining.*

"I was watchin dis show, dis boy reminded me so much of you."

"I love you, GG. The phone gonna hang up."

"I love y—"

The call was cut off before GG could finish saying "I love you." Possible hated ending the call like that, but didn't have enough time to call back, so he just held the phone to his ear and heard GG's voice in his head: "I love you too, baby."

As Possible hung up the phone he was surprised to see the Jpay open, but then again everyone was still at work and school. Checking his messages, he found pics from Charlie and Sabrina along with two VideoGrams.

The dayroom intercom blasted: "Five minutes till dayroom's closed! Dayroom closed in five minutes!

Rushing to download the VideoGrams, Possible didn't have time to view them while they downloaded to his tablet.

I'll just watch 'em when I get back to the cell, he thought.

"Dayroom closed!" Dayroom's over! Cell in!"

Possible was in no rush to cell in, he was still downloading.

"Jenkins, let's go, cell in," CO Peters ordered.

"I got one minute left to finish downloadin, Possible replied.

CO Peters walked over to see if Possible was lying.

"What you downloadin?" Peters asked.

"Couple VideoGrams from my girl."

"Is your girl white?" CO Peters asked.

"Yeah, she white." Possible showed Peters a pic while he finished downloading, confused, not understanding why it mattered if she was white.

"I know how you brothers love them white women."

"'You brothers?' Ain't you Black too?" Possible asked.

"Yeah, but I never dated a white woman."

"What, workin out here wit all these white people and you ain't…?"

Out of respect, Possible didn't finish the sentence. He'd been caught up in the moment, and the question had just come out.

"I been married for twenty-three years to a beautiful Black queen, Peters answered proudly.

"I heard you and Peters was best friends, so I thought you grew up out here."

"Naw, I'm from Compton, California. I came to Washington in the early eighties, me and wifey. CO Peters coo. He from Cali too. He married to a Sistah," Peters replied in a secretive tone.

"I knew somethin was different bout CO Peters; he got a different type of swag," Possible replied.

Getting up from the Jpay, Possible started to head back to the cell.

"Jenkins, that stays between us," Peters said.

"What's understood don't have to be said," Possible replied.

CO Peters just smiled and walked away. While Possible was on the Jpay, Sweaty was in the cell window watching the two converse.

"What you download?" Sweaty asked, as Possible entered the cell.

"VideoGrams baby sent me."

"Let me see!"

"Hold up, my nigga, I ain't even seen 'em yet," Possible snapped.

"You and CO Peters was choppin it up."

"Yeah, he's aight," Possible replied, checking out the VideoGrams.

"What was he talkin bout?" Sweaty asked.

"Shit, talkin bout how us Blacks love white women."

"Like he ain't Black hisself," Sweaty said.

"Damn!" Possible said, watching the VideoGram of Sabrina twerking. He'd never known thirty seconds could feel like an eternity.

"Let me see?" Sweaty asked.

"My bad, my nigga, but not this one, this is baby," but Possible teased him with a quick peek.

"Oh, shit! I'm bout to tell baby to send me one," Sweaty said. "I ain't gonna lie, my girl ain't got a ass like that," he added.

Possible just smiled with pride.

"You really do have a thing for thick white girls," Sweaty said.

"I told you they do something to me, I can't explain it," Possible said, replaying the video.

"What's up is it's bout to be count. Let's roll," Sweaty said.

"Go 'head, it's your shit," Possible replied, staying focused on the video.

"So if I'm askin you to roll, that means what?" Sweaty asked, irritated at his sweaty condition.

"Ha-ha, I got you, my nigga." Possible reluctantly put the tablet away and began to roll. "You stretchin this cap, he said, dumping enough to roll a nice fat stick.

"You gotta know what you doin," Sweaty replied.

"'Bout two, three more sticks left," Possible said, handing Sweaty the little plastic bag.

"We should be on by the time it's all gone?" Sweaty asked, trying to disguise the question as a statement.

Possible didn't want to give the exact day when the pack would arrive. "Hopefully," he answered, putting the final touches on the stick.

"They should be doin count any—"

"Count! Standing Count! You must be standing or sitting!"

"Any minute!" Sweaty finished with a smile.

Possible shut off the video, and the TV came on. "You got the lighter and shit ready?" he asked.

Sweaty looked at him with a big cheesy grin.

"Why did I ask you that?" Possible said. He knew what was coming from the moment the words left his mouth.

"I'm Sweaty, and I stay ready!" Sweaty said. "They bout to walk by right now," he added, as he and Possible waited for the guards to go by.

"Breaking news!" the TV announced. Another deadly police shooting of an unarmed Black man. What started as a routine traffic stop ended in a fatal shooting caught on the officer's body cam.

"What the fuck! Turn this up." Sweaty said.

"We are going to show you the fatal shooting, but we must warn you the images are disturbing and not suitable for small children to watch."

"Oh, shit, my nigga!" Sweaty blurted.

"Damn, he didn't even give him a chance!" Possible snapped.

"We're Black men in America. We don't get a chance or the benefit of the doubt," Sweaty said, feeling sad for the man he'd just seen lose his life.

"It's crazy how this terrorist blew some shit up the other day, he's runnin through the streets of New York wit a fake gun in the middle of the afternoon, and police find a way to take him alive—gunshot to the leg and shit," Possible said angrily. "This nigga sittin in his car, refused to roll his windows all the way down but still gave the police his license and shit."

"You don't have to roll your window all the way down, just enough to give them your license," Sweaty added.

"Did they walk by yet?" That shit got me hot!" Possible said.

"Yeah, we good," Sweaty said, feeling somber, but their mood began to change as the two smoked.

"That's why niggas don't fuck with the police!" Possible said, inhaling and exhaling a bunch of smoke and passing the stick to Sweaty.

"Oh, yeah, that ain't what it looked like earlier when you was choppin it up wit officer Peters," Sweaty teased, exhaling his own cloud and passing the stick back.

"One, Officer Peters ain't a police officer, and two, just cause you see me converse wit someone don't mean I fuck wit 'im," Possible said defensively.

"What the hell is 'converse'? And you never told me what you and CO Peters was talkin bout. I heard him say that stays between me and you."

"If you heard him say that, then why would you ask me what he said? Did you hear him say tell Sweaty too?"

"Give me my stick!" Sweaty demanded.

"Oh, and 'converse' is the proper term for talk, short for conversation," Possible teased, taking another hit before passing the stick. "I'm fuckin wit you. We was just talkin bout where he from, and CO Peters is married to a Black woman."

"I already knew that, and Peters from Compton," Sweaty said.

"Well there you go, nosy," Possible replied.

"You got to know your personnel, know who's who round here. How else you s'posed to get an advantage?" Sweaty asked. "I see you startin to catch on, gettin the logistics."

"I'm just adaptin to my environment, that's all." Possible said, grabbing the end of the roach from Sweaty, who said, "We need to make sure we play our cards right wit this Dam'on situation!"

"What you mean?" Possible asked, finishing the roach and flushing the rest.

"I'm just sayin we can really make shit happen reachin down to J-unit. We need to reach down there."

"I don't know nobody down there," Possible said.

"I do, Matt do, we just need to find somebody we can trust that works in the kitchen.

"J-money the only nigga I know and trust," Possible said.

"He'll never work, he's Dam'on's number one. How you think Dam'on reaches down there."

"We need to get in the kitchen," Possible said.

"We can't, because of the riot back at W.R.C. You got to be cross quad approved, and we not," Sweaty said.

"Matt was just tellin me how he been waitin to get in there." Possible replied.

"Let's hope he get it, then we on for real!"

"You never been to J-unit?" Possible asked.

"Yeah, it's coo, just different politics," Sweaty said. "What time is it? I just seen the guards walk by doin count again."

"Recount. It's gonna be a minute till count clears. We might as well roll another one," Possible said.

"Fuck it, might as well," Sweaty agreed. "I got it, I ain't sweaty right now."

"You should get that looked at," Possible said.

"I know, but I don't want them to tell me I got cancer or somethin," Sweaty said.

"What, you wouldn't wanna know if you had somethin could kill you?"

"Nope, I wanna just die. If I know, then everybody be all sad and shit. I already live life like it's my last anyway," Sweaty replied, twisting the stick.

"Yeah, but yo family might wanna see you more, or yo girl."

"See, that's the fucked-up part: bein sick get you more sympathy. You should wanna see me more, but I got to be sick for you to wanna see me more," Sweaty said, sparking the stick.

Possible understood what Sweaty was saying. If you cared, it shouldn't matter if somebody was sick or not. "I feel you on that one," he shot back.

"Fuck it, we all gotta go one day," Sweaty replied, sucking down a cloud of smoke.

Possible! Possible! Sweaty!

"Ay, somebody callin us!"

"Possible!"

"What's good? asked Sweaty, yelling through the door and passing Possible the stick.

"Ay! Make sure y'all go to mainline, cause ain't no dayroom on account of recount!"

"Who is that?" Sweaty asked, not recognizing the voice.

"Matt!"

"Aight, don't trip," Sweaty answered.

"This nigga actin like we was the ones sleepin this mornin," Possible said, passing the stick back.

"He just tryna see what's up wit smoke, that's what. Watch, I bet he gonna ask for a stick." Sweaty said, passing the roach to Possible.

"I'm good, go 'head," Possible said.

"He prob'ly smellin it too," Sweaty replied.

The booth officer announced: "Count's clear! Prepare for mainline! Count's clear!"

Chapter 12

What Do the Homies Call You?

As the three made their way back from mainline, Matt found the perfect opportunity. "Y'all know we ain't gonna have dayroom, right. It's already 6:50, and they stop runnin dayroom at 7:00." Matt said, setting up the play.

"We already figured that much," Sweaty said, giving Possible a wink when Matt wasn't looking.

"We should be good tomorrow, huh?" Matt asked, in reference to getting the pack.

" I hope. That's what I was told," Possible replied, giving Sweaty the look.

"Look, lemme get a stick till then," Matt asked.

"Ha-ha-ha-ha! What I tell you! Possible and Sweaty burst out laughing, which left Matt looking confused.

"What's so funny? Can I laugh too?" he asked.

"Naw, look," Possible said. "When you yelled out askin us to go to mainline, Sweaty said, 'He just want smoke, wait and see.'" The two burst into laughter again.

"Since you knew what I was gonna ask, did you bring me a stick?"

Yeah, I got you, my nigga," Sweaty said, handing Matt a piece of plastic.

"My nigga," Matt replied with a smile.

As the three made it back to the unit, Possible noticed two COs he'd never seen before. He knew these dudes were different because their aura screamed power and importance. They were dressed in plain clothes, with gold badges around their necks.

"What's up, Matt?" Administrator Frazier said in a friendly tone. "Haven't seen or heard from you lately. Staying out of trouble?"

"I must be, if you ain't seen me," Matt replied.

"Hanging out with Sweaty now, huh? Who's the new guy?" Frazier asked, chewing hard on his gum. Possible just ignored him.

"Hey! I asked you a question. Yeah, I'm talkin to you."

Possible tried to look confused.

"What's your name?" Frazier asked.

"Jenkins," Possible answered.

Frazier just smiled. "Naw, that's what people who don't know any better call you. What do the homies call you?"

Possible just stared in disbelief, He'd never been challenged so blatantly, especially by a CO—or whoever Frazier was.

"Relax, I'm just teasing," Frazier said, smiling along with his partner at the fact that he had rattled Possible.

"Look, it's a good thing I don't know what the homies call you. Try to keep it that way. You gentlemen enjoy the rest of your evening." Frazier and his partner stayed in the unit while the three walked back to their cells. Matt and Sweaty were cool about the situation, but Possible was obviously shaken.

"My nigga, what the fuck was that?" Possible asked when they were out of earshot of Frazier.

"It's coo, he be power trippin. Just ignore it," Matt answered.

"I tried that. It got worse," Possible said.

"Aight, in the mornin," Matt replied. When they reached his cell, he shook Sweaty's and Possible's hands. "Don't trip, you prob'ly won't see him again," Matt said, entering his cell.

Possible and Sweaty walked a few doors farther down and waited for their cell door to open.

"Hold up," Sweaty said. "Ima cover the speaker when we get inside," meaning the cell intercom. "Man, who's playin tonight?" he asked, pretending to be interested in a game, though his intention was to throw off the COs if they were listening.

"You already know. Kobe!" Possible replied, playing along.

"Kobe! Oh, hell no, Kobe been retired three years ago." Sweaty said, laughing at Possible's lack of sports knowledge. As the two continued to talk sports, Sweaty was preparing to cover the speaker. He grabbed a bunch of tissue, dampened it in water, and smashed it against the speaker, creating a suction as the wet tissue stuck.

"Look, wit Administrator Frazier you gotta keep your cool at all times. He likes to fish info outta you, tease, ask a question just to see what type of reaction he can get."

"Well, if I wasn't high as a kite it prob'ly wouldn't a been a big deal," Possible replied.

"You aight. I'm not in the mix like that, so you bein wit me he knows you aight," Sweaty said.

"Bullshit! He knew you and Matt's aliases!" Possible snapped.

"Yeah, cause they got me down as S.T.G."

"What's S.T.G?"

"Security Threat Group. They think I run the City G," Sweaty said.

"Why they think that?"

"Snitches, watchin who you hang wit, listenin to phone conversations, checkin tattoos, but mostly snitches."

"What bout Matt?"

"Shit, Matt been down for twenty years, so I'm sure over his time he ran across Frazier a few times. Shit, Frazier was prob'ly just a regular CO when Matt first came through the joint," Sweaty said. "Look, you only need to worry bout Frazier when somebody gettin stabbed. That's prob'ly why he was here, for that stabbin."

"That was three months ago."

"You know how long an investigation can take? As long as they want, specially when it was that bad."

Possible was taking in all this information, making a mental note that he never wanted to run into Frazier. The man had the *I'll fuck you over* type of aura.

"Don't trip. Like I said, you prob'ly won't ever see him again. Let's roll," Sweaty suggested.

"Are you good to twist?" Possible asked.

"Yeah." Sweaty pulled out the last of the smoke and began to roll. Possible got the lighter ready.

"We go to yard in the mornin, right?" Possible asked.

"Uh, yeah." Sweaty answered.

"Why you say it like that?"

"You forgot bout D-man and all that shit."

"Oh, yeah, Zay gonna owe me ten bucks for that."

"I wanted Zay to do that cause this nigga I Like It Here be goin overboard."

"What you mean, 'overboard'?" Possible asked.

"Ain't no tellin wit this nigga. You thinkin it's a head-up fade, next thing you know he fightin the police or fightin somebody he's not supposed be fightin."

"He looks like he likes that shit too."

"He do, I guarantee you. Zay was still gonna do it, but he talked Zay out of it, usin the visit as his advantage. We should be good, though, cause it's one of our own. I just hope he don't trip wit the police."

"You gonna have to let him know," Possible replied.

"I know. Did they walk by yet?"

"Yeah," Possible answered.

As the two smoked, Sweaty got relaxed. So did Possible, forgetting about his encounter with Administrator Frazier. Inhale, exhale, with every puff they both felt more comfortable—an ease that would be cut short by tomorrow morning's events. As the two called it an early night, Possible thinking about the drop with the laundry and Sweaty thinking about the D-man situation, they both understood, each in his own way, that tomorrow was a big day, but the results would be something neither one was prepared for.

* * *

The following morning, to his surprise, Sweaty awoke to Possible brushing his teeth.

"Damn, hell done froze over," Sweaty said, jumping off the top bunk.

"Oh, yeah, hell gonna get used to freezin, cause things is gonna be this way," Possible replied.

"Is that right?" Sweaty asked.

"That's right!" Possible said.

"Yeah, aight. Watch out, let me piss," Sweaty said.

Possible washed the remainder of the toothpaste out of his mouth, and sat on his bunk so Sweaty could pee.

"Did they do count yet?" Sweaty asked.

"Yeah, they just turned the count light off right before you got up."

"Aight, let me get ready. Man, I had a dream that Zay and this nigga I Like It Here jumped D-man at mainline.

"I hope not," Possible replied. "That would fuck up the drop; two on one, that's a lockdown," he added.

"I know, but Zay got visit today, so I know that not gonna happen."

"Is I Like It Here that unpredictable that he got you dreamin and shit?" Possible asked, while Sweaty brushed his teeth. "I'm sure if you talk to him he'll just beat 'im up."

"That shit don't matter. Clearly he fucked up, so I Like It Here ain't gonna view him as of one of our own," Sweaty replied, spitting out a mouthful of toothpaste and water.

"We good. Ay, turn to *First Take*," Sweaty demanded.

"I'm watchin CNN," Possible replied.

"They gonna be showin the same news shit all day. Why you gotta be so difficult?" Sweaty asked.

Possible just smiled. He knew this was Sweaty's morning routine, but he just wanted to get a reaction from his cellie.

"Good-lookin, bro!" Sweaty said, as Possible began to change the channel. "You know what I just realized? It's Saturday. No mainline this mornin," Sweaty announced.

"I knew somethin was funny bout this mornin," Possible said. "They bout to call yard in a minute."

"I know," Sweaty replied as he put on his sweats and shoes.

"That's coo too. I can holla at Dam'on while we out there," Possible said.

"I'm missin somethin: how you gonna holla at Dam'on and make the drop if he's at the yard?" Sweaty asked.

"I don't know. Why you keep tryna fish for the move? I told you it's good, he don't want nobody to know," Possible said.

"I know," Sweaty said. I guess I'm tryna solve the puzzle. I always wondered how this nigga was gettin it. He's filthy, he been moving like this for a minute now, so whatever the system is, it's workin."

"That's why when we go out I can get the details bout when." Possible said, already knowing the details.

"H-unit! Prepare for Yard! H-unit, Yard!"

On the way to yard, Possible's heart was racing, not because of the potential fight but the way Sweaty hyped it up, how I Like It Here could be so unpredictable.

What if I have to get involved? Possible thought, knowing at the same time that this was City G's handling City G business. There was no need for him or anyone else to get involved.

We'll be aight, Possible thought, as he, Matt, and Sweaty entered the yard.

"Ay, what's happenin?" I Like It Here asked, greeting the three.

"What's good, my nigga!" Sweaty asked.

"Shit, chillin, ready to mix some shit," I Like It Here replied.

"Did D-man come out?" Sweaty asked.

"Yeah, he over there wit some niggas, waitin to talk to you."

"Shit I forgot all bout y'all little soap-opera shit," Matt snapped.

"Make sure you let Zay know he owes me ten bucks," Possible said.

"I'm not gonna see Zay for a minute," I Like It Here replied. This gave Sweaty an uneasy feeling; he knew by the way I Like It Here said he wasn't gonna see Zay for a minute that it was gonna be bad.

"Oh, yeah, I forgot bout that. I'm bout to holla at Dam'on," Possible replied, feeling like an airhead.

"I'm comin wit you!" Matt announced.

"Tell D-man I wanna holla at 'im," Sweaty said with a blank stare.

The three men went their separate ways, Possible and Matt toward the Burgundy B's and I Like It Here to retrieve D-man.

"You know I'm bout to talk to Dam'on bout business?" Possible asked Matt.

"I know. I was just tryna not be over there when all that shit happens," Matt replied.

"I don't blame you. Hold up, I'll be back," Possible said, while walking up on the group of Burgundy B's.

"Possible, what's good?" Dam'on asked.

"Shit. What's good wit you?" Possible asked as the two shook hands.

"I thought maybe you'd be stayin back. You know the drop's bein made right now," Dam'on said.

"They passin out laundry while we at yard?" Possible asked.

"Yeah. I had it set up like that so you had some privacy while you put it together," Dam'on replied.

"Damn, I thought—never mind," Possible said, stopping himself from giving an excuse.

"It's all good. Nobody knows, That's why I told you not to tell anybody, so when you do shit like come to yard instead of waiting on the drop, you have room for error. The bag should already be sittin in front of your door. Don't open it in front of Sweaty," Dam'on cautioned.

"I got you. Once the source is compromised, the operation is compromised," Possible replied, letting Dam'on know he'd been listening.

The animated siren went off in the big yard. "Down on the ground! Inmates, get on the ground!" boomed over the loudspeakers.

Guards rushed into the yard. "Stop fighting!" they shouted.

The fight had slipped Possible's mind for a split second. On his stomach, along with Dam'on, he could see that this was more than a fight. D-man's body lay bloody and unmoving. Possible's heart began to race again. His eyes quickly searched for Sweaty, and found him on his stomach by the phones. As the guards cuffed I Like It Here, it was clear as day.

"Well, we bout to go on lockdown," Dam'on announced, having seen the same thing Possible had. Blood was dripping from I Like It Here's right hand, and some type of shank lay by D-man's head.

"Fuck! When you get back, make sure you grab the laundry bag, It should be right in front—the bag wit the orange tag is the one; the other is just your regular laundry bag."

"Everybody gonna have laundry in front of their door, right?" Possible asked.

"Yeah, but sometimes they get the cells mixed up, that's why I said look for the orange tag."

As Dam'on went over the instructions for the drop, Possible made eye contact with I Like It Here. Time began to slow down; everything moved in slow motion. I Like It Here's smile reminded Possible of the smile from the white guy who'd done the stabbing in the dayroom, which gave Possible another flashback to Benny.

"Possible! Possible!" Dam'on yelled. He had to shake Possible in order to get him to snap back.

"Yeah, the orange tag," Possible responded, coming back to reality.

"You good, my nigga?" Dam'on asked.

"I'm good, got lost for a minute, that's all."

As a medical team rushed the stretcher carrying D-man's body out of the yard, Dam'on took a second to ask, "Ay, did somebody close to you die in your case?"

"Yeah, my best friend," Possible said.

"You saw the whole thing, huh?"

"Yeah."

"Damn, I'm sorry to hear that."

"It's all good. He had to die," Possible replied with a blank stare. Dam'on wasn't prepared for that type of response. He realized it was deeper than he'd imagined, so he decided to let go of the subject.

"So. we good on everythin? We gonna be on lockdown when we get back, so just try and make it look like you got the pack out here if Sweaty asks," Dam'on said.

"How long you think we gonna be on lockdown?" Possible asked.

"We not comin out for a least few days, but because it was the same race, that's in our favor. The white-boy stabbing, the unit was on lockdown for two days," Dam'on added, giving Possible hope.

"Wasn't the reason the white boy got stabbed was cause he was a CI?" Possible asked.

"Yep. Administration knew he was a confidential informant and left him on mainline anyway, so they partly to blame for that," Dam'on said.

"That's fucked up," Possible replied.

"Administration don't care bout none of that. We all pieces of shit in their eyes," Dam'on said.

"How long we gonna be out here on the ground?" As Possible asked this the guards began to escort inmates out of the yard one by one.

"We gonna be here for a minute. They doin one-by-one escorts wit zip-ties and shit," Dam'on answered.

Well, kick back. I'm bout to enjoy this extended weekend," Possible said with a satisfied grin.

"Now you see why I said, 'Don't let Sweaty drive,'" Dam'on said.

"Yeah. Last night he was stressin bout how I Like It Here was gonna handle business."

"He shoulda had one of his li'l City G's handle D-man," Dam'on said, "and kept I Like It Here for the real shit, cause every now and then it gets real roun here."

When the guards picked Matt up to escort him back to the unit, he wasn't that far from Possible and Dam'on.

"I still don't get all this politics shit," Possible said.

"It's really not all that difficult if mothafuckas handle their own," Dam'on replied.

Possible looked across the yard to see Sweaty make eye contact with him, shaking his head in disbelief.

"We bout to get outta here, we next," Dam'on said. "I put all the info in the bag, and the joog that's in your unit," Dam'on added, as he could see the guards coming for Possible.

"Put your hands behind your back," one of the guards ordered. Possible complied, got zip-tied, then stood up and said a last good-bye to Dam'on. Possible was escorted back to the unit, where he figured he had enough time to get the pack before his cellie got back. *Worked out aight,* Possible thought.

Chapter 13

Forbidden Three

In the three days since the stabbing, Possible had been in the cell by himself, wondering what they had taken Sweaty for. It was obvious he wasn't involved physically, so maybe conspiracy? Possible remembered Sweaty saying Administration had him as the leader.

A CO popped up out of nowhere and ordered, "Jenkins, come to the door and cuff up." Possible's heart was pounding so hard it felt like he could see it through his shirt. As he came to the door he saw four guards standing outside the door.

"What's goin on?" Possible asked.

"We're conducting a Forbidden 3-violation extraction," the CO explained.

With his butt cheeks stuffed with marijuana, Possible thought about covering the cell window and flushing the smoke, but instead decided to turn around and cuff up. He put his hands through the cuff board of the cell door, and once he was cuffed, the door slid open.

* * *

"All right, Jenkins, I need you to have a seat at this table," the CO ordered.

While Possible sat at the table, he noticed another four guards doing the extraction at Matt's cell.

Another CO ordered, "All right, Mr. Richardson, have a seat next to Mr. Jenkins." Matt had gone through this procedure a hundred times. He and Possible were left alone while the guards did a quick cell search.

"What the hell is all this?" Possible asked.

"Damn!" Matt replied.

"We goin to the hole?" Possible asked, nervous about getting stripped and searched.

"Naw, but they bout to take a bunch of our shit from us."

"For what?" We ain't do nothin!" Possible exclaimed.

"It's Forbidden 3. If someone you fuck wit commit a Forbidden 3, they can take yo shit," Matt explained.

"They can do that?"

"They doin it," Matt shot back.

"All right, gentlemen, here's a copy of the violation and your restrictions," The CO said, holding the TV and shoes in one hand and the paperwork in the other.

"You got *my* shoes; those ain't my cellie's," Possible said.

"I know. No shoes, no TV, and no big yard are part of your restrictions for the violations," the officer explained.

"But I ain't commit no violation," Possible said.

"Hey, I just do what I'm told. Your name and Mr. Richardson's are on the list. The restrictions are for thirty days, and any violation can result in disciplinary action," the CO said. This authoritative tone made Possible realize his butt cheeks were filled with smoke.

"Whatever," Possible replied.

"Ain't no use of arguing wit 'em. That only makes it worse," Matt said.

"All right, you two, stand up and head back to the cell."

The two complied and the cuffs were taken off through the cuff board.

"Ay, Jenkins, you wanna pack all your cellie's property, we'll be back to get it."

"My cellie ain't comin back?" Possible asked.

"I don't know. I was told to get his property, so doesn't seem like it," the CO replied.

Feeling a sense of relief at not being strip-searched, but also despairing for Sweaty, Possible counted his blessings and began to pack Sweaty's belongings.

* * *

Three weeks passed since the CO had come and taken Sweaty's property. Possible and Matt had only a week left on Forbidden 3.

"Man, I can't wait. I been goin crazy in the cell, talkin to myself, creatin movie scenes and shit," Possible said.

"I'm surprised they ain't give you a cellie!" Matt replied as he washed the dominos.

"You think they gonna bring Sweaty back to my cell?" Possible asked.

"I dunno. Word in the kitchen is they haven't gave 'im his writeup yet," Matt said, pushing the dominos to Possible to give him the choice to pick his bones first.

"I hope so, even though he act retarded sometimes, that's still my guy," Possible said, picking up seven bones.

"Ay, whatever happen to da shit?" Matt asked.

"I got it," Possible answered coolly.

"For real, did it get pushed back because of the situation in the yard?" Matt asked.

"I got it. I'm sittin on it right now. Put me on, that's fifteen." Possible replied, slapping his double bone on a blank three bone. Matt just stared at Possible as if he hadn't heard him count fifteen.

"What's good? You gonna put me on?" Possible asked.

"Nigga, you gonna put *me* on!"

" I know you ain't have pack this whole time, we ain't been nowhere," Matt said.

"I got it the same day all that shit happen, I got spooked when they came with that Forbidden 3 shit." Possible explained. Matt continued to stare at Possible with disbelief.

"I just figured we can bust down when we got off that shit. I don't want them poppin up on a nigga," Possible explained.

"If you don't bust that shit down, ain't nobody comin back, when the thirty days is up CO Peters and Peters gonna give us our shit back." Matt explained.

"Can I get my fifteen?"

"Fuck these dominos! Nigga, I been stressin. No TV, no big yard, and the whole time the shit is a couple doors down," Matt said, frustrated.

"You think we good?" Possible asked.

"I'm bout to come across this table on you if you don't go and bust that shit down."

"Aight, let's finish this game," Possible replied with a cheap grin.

"Fuck this game! I'm bout to lock down and get my line ready," Matt said.

"Aight, I'm gonna use the phone for the fifteen minutes," Possible said.

"You still got that line from lockdown?" Matt asked, meaning the dental floss used as a fishing line to transport things from cell to cell when the unit was on lockdown and the cell doors weren't allowed to open.

"I got you," Possible answered on his way to the phone.

"What's up, baby? Took you long enough to call," Sabrina said after pressing 5 to accept the call.

"We been on lockdown. Did you take care of that?" Possible asked.

"Yeah."

"Did you do it just like I told you wit the money app?"

"Yes, baby, everythin all taken care of, just like you wanted it."

"When you comin back up?"

"I'm tryna see what's up wit Maddy—her and Charlie still beefin."

"Bout what?"

"Dayroom closed. Cell in!" Dayroom closed"

"Ay, Ima call you tomorrow."

"You just called. We got ten minutes left," Sabrina snapped.

"I know, but I gotta lock down. Ima call tomorrow, I promise. I love you."

"Promise?"

"Promise."

"Love you, daddy." Sabrina said, as Possible rushed off the phone to go back to his cell. With the Forbidden 3 almost over, he didn't want to take any chances, especially with the smoke on him.

"Matt!… Matt!" Possible yelled once he'd gotten back in his cell.

"Yeah, I'm ready!" Matt shouted back.

"Ay, Ima shoot you a few shots of coffee till we figure it out," Possible explained, referring to the smoke as coffee, so other inmates wouldn't know he was talking about marijuana.

"Yep!" Matt yelled. Using his fingernail clippers as a weight tied to the dental floss, Possible threw the clippers hard as he could under his cell door.

"Stay right there!" Matt yelled, seeing the floss in front of his cell. Instead of nail clippers, Matt used a hair comb so its teeth could grab the floss while he pulled the line into his cell.

"Got it!" Matt yelled.

"Aight, hold up!" Possible said, needing time to tie the smoke to the line. "Go ahead, pull!"

"Yep, good lookin, bro!" Matt yelled as he pulled the smoke into his cell.

"Tomorrow we'll figure everythin out!" Possible said.

"Aight! Have a good night."

"Yep. G'night, bro!"

Possible sat alone, looking at the pile of smoke, thinking about what would be the best way to make the most money. Dam'on only charged him $1,000 for the whole twenty-eight grams, and Sabrina just confirmed that everything was paid for. Now he needed to at the least double his money. Remembering what Sweaty had taught him about the Chapstick, Possible began to measure out caps. The COs had already done count, and it was midnight shift, so Possible felt comfortable measuring out caps. He can hear Sweaty's voice in his head now: Always wait till graveyard shift; that way you don't have to worry bout them openin the cell door—it's quiet, and you can hear the unit door open."

Possible smiled at hearing Sweaty's voice. He would make sure Sweaty was on as soon as he gets back, he told himself. Possible rolled a stick and began to smoke while measuring the caps. He got forty-five, and at $75 apiece he was guaranteed to double if not triple his money. With Matt in the kitchen being able to reach other units, Possible figured why not try to find someone to pick up the whole twenty-eight and let *them* deal with the caps, except with that idea he wouldn't get as much as he would dealing caps. This could be the conversation he would have with Matt over breakfast. Inhaling a huge cloud of smoke, Possible grinned at the thought that his plans were coming together.

Chapter 14

This Gang Shit is For the Birds

The following morning Possible and Matt sat at the breakfast table and went over the order of the operation.

"I'm not tryna be sittin on this shit like that," Possible said, scooping a bite of biscuit and gravy into his mouth.

"Shit, you ain't got to. I got a spot where we can keep it," Matt replied.

"Where at?"

"In the kitchen. There's a room where we can put it in the ceilin."

"How many people know bout the ceilin?"

"You think I'd stash somethin where everybody knows?"

"Why you think you the only one knows' bout this spot?" Possible asked.

"cause nobody but me and another person is allowed back there, and the other person is a square white boy who don't know nothin." Matt explained, taking a bite of his breakfast.

"Aight."

"Look, we bust it down in caps, sell $85 apiece and kill 'em like that. I'm tellin you they gonna move like hotcakes, Matt said with a smile. The two men saw Zay approaching and changed topics.

"I told you they don't know when Sweaty getting' out?" Matt said.

"What's good? Who don't know when Sweaty gettin out?" Zay asked, taking a seat at the table.

"Naw, we ain't goin for that," Possible said. Where my ten bucks at? We almost off Forbidden 3 and you still ain't paid me."

"As long as I owe you you'll never be broke," Zay said jokingly. "They said Sweaty gettin a program," he announced. "I got you two on store day in a couple days."

"What they give Sweaty a program for?" Possible asked.

"I don't know. Prob'ly just bein STG," Zay answered.

"I try to tell y'all that gang shit for the birds. Niggas too old to be talkin bout 'my big homey.' Niggas 'round here thirty, thirty-five years old, talkin bout 'I just got put on, my big homie told me to do this or that,' you niggas sound silly," Matt said.

"What a nigga need to do is get this money!" Possible said.

"So what's up? Sweaty was talkin bout some shit with some move?" Zay asked.

"Yeah, we bout to put it together. Don't even trip, we got you," Possible replied.

"Richardson and Jenkins, time's up!" the chow hall CO boomed.

"Ay, make sure you come to yard when we get off this shit—and have ten bucks too!" Possible demanded as he left the table along with Matt.

"Aight, Boss," Zay replied, mocking Possible's ordering him around.

Walking back to the unit, Possible felt good about the new plan. *Matt came through*, he thought. As the two entered the unit, smiles on their faces, it was time to put the play in motion.

* * *

Two weeks later: "What's good, baby?" Possible asked Sabrina.

"Uh, just sittin here waitin on your people."

"Where you at?"

"Down by the McDonald's and Safeway."

"In Juanita?" Possible asked, shivering, regretting that he hadn't brought his jacket.

"Yeah, and if they're not here in fifteen minutes, I'm leavin!" Sabrina snapped.

"Calm down, they gonna be there," Possible said. "How much bread you got altogether so far?" he asked.

"There bout a band—$1,000—and some change."

This put a smile on Possible's face. In two weeks he was already seeing the play working out, with a band in the bank another $800–$900 out that he was waiting to collect, and he was expecting a drop this week. Things were coming along just as planned.

"Aight, look when… matter of fact, call Charlie on three-way," Possible ordered.

"Hold up. Your people just text me they're here," Sabrina replied with attitude.

Joker walked up and asked, "Ay, Possible when you get off the phone, can I holla at you?"

Possible just nodded, as he was trying to listen to Sabrina.

"Aight, baby?"

"I'm here," Possible answered.

"I'm bout to call Charlie," Sabrina snapped.

Possible could hear the attitude in her voice as he waited for Charlie to answer.

"Yep!" Charlie said.

"Peety! My guy," Possible shot back.

"Look, I don't have a lot of time left out here in the yard, but Sabrina got a couple bucks for you. Baby, shoot that band to Charlie and hold on to everythin else."

"What you got goin on?" Charlie asked, suspicious.

"Baby had a couple extra bucks from the club. I just told her to shoot it to you for GG's medical bills. I talked to GG a few weeks ago, and she said she been in and out the hospital."

"Yeah, but I told you everythins taken care of. I got it!" Charlie snapped.

Trying to keep his composure, Possible said, "Look, my nigga, you ain't God. Take the fuckin money and pay GG's medical bills or BJ's, and stop actin like everythins good when it ain't. Sabrina got a few extra dollars, I'm glad we can help in some way!"

Charlie took a moment to respond, admiring his best friend, his little brother's big heart. "Aight I just wanna make sure you're not fuckin up."

This was the closest Possible would get to a thank-you for the help, and also let him know that Charlie really did need help, just like Maddy had said.

"I got you, my nigga!" Possible said with pride. "Sabrina—

The robot voice interrupted: You have sixty seconds remaining!"

"Ima slide through later tonight," Charlie said.

Sabrina shot back, "I'm bout to pick Maddy up from work. I'll just give the cash to her."

"Thirty seconds remaining!"

"Y'all figure it out. I love y'all. Baby, call you later."

"What bout, my nigga?" Charlie said, jokingly.

"I got you!"

As the call ended, Possible had a smile on his face. A sense of fulfilment motivated him even more.

Joker... Ay, Joker!

Chapter 15

Ima Turn Your Water On

Back in the unit, Possible and Matt were discussing business over a game of dominos.

"Big six, five, four?"

"I got big four!" Matt said, laying down a double four.

"How much left?" Possible asked, laying down his domino.

"Shit, I dunno, bout five, six caps," Matt said.

"Aight. We should be gettin another drop soon, but Joker tryna get two, so when you go back to work, make sure you grab two."

"Ima grab three, cause I got a joog too," Matt replied.

"Yup, ten! Put me on board!" Possible exclaimed, slamming the domino.

"Ay, and tell your people don't be havin baby waitin like that. She gets hella upset, then she take it out on me."

"My bad. My brother a slowpoke," Matt said.

"That ain't gonna work. We need to figure out a different system," Possible replied, laying down another domino.

"That's fifteen!" Matt called out.

Suddenly there was a commotion among the inmates in the unit. One of them shouted, "Sweaty comin into the unit!" which grabbed the attention of Possible and Matt.

"Sweaty walkin on the breezeway to the unit right now!" the same inmate said.

Possible got up to look out the window, but from his viewpoint, he couldn't see anybody.

"How you know it's Sweaty?" Possible asked the inmate.

"Man. I been knowin Sweaty for years. I know his walk from anybody's," the man said.

"Come on, we bout to see in a minute, it's on you." Matt said with attitude.

"What's wrong wit you? Sweaty's back—that's our guy," Possible said joyfully.

Matt forced a fake smile. "I know. I'm just tryna get my action back. I'm tired of you whippin my ass," Matt shot back.

Possible sat down accepting the excuse, but noticed Matt's jealousy even more.

"It's gonna be aight, there enough for us to bust down three ways. Sweaty ain't gonna dip into your cut," Possible said in a half-joking way.

"Naw, Sweaty's my nigga," Matt said, smiling at the fact that Possible was right.

The booth officer announced: "Five minutes till dayroom is closed! Five minutes! Dayroom is over!"

"See what I mean? Now I can't catch you cause dayroom's closed," Matt groused.

"Keep the score if it means that much to you," Possible replied, watching the unit door for Sweaty.

"Naw, you got it. We'll start a new game later," Matt said, conceding.

"Aight, don't forget to grab that! Possible reminded Matt about the smoke.

"I ain't goin to work right this minute," Matt snapped, as he celled in.

As the last of the inmates returned to their cells, Possible stood at his cell window, waiting to see if Sweaty would walk through the doors. After a couple of minutes Possible realized that Sweaty wasn't coming back after all. Zay said he had been put on a program meant to improve his behavior, and to Possible's knowledge, programs lasted six months to a year. It'd been only three and a half months since the stabbing. Possible sat on his bunk and was flipping through channels when he heard a commotion outside his cell.

"What's up, my nigga?!"

Possible recognized Sweaty's voice.

"Sweaty!" Possible heard someone yell, confirming he was right. As he got up to see, Possible cell door began to open startling Possible before he could catch Sweaty coming in the cell.

"What's up my nigga!" Possible greeted Sweaty excitedly. With his long hair, Sweaty looked like Tom Hanks in *Cast Away*. Sweaty just pushed past Possible without embracing him or speaking.

"Damn, my nigga like that," Possible said, his hurt feelings obvious in his voice as the cell door closed.

"I'm just fuckin wit you, my nigga!" Sweaty said with *I got you!* delight. Possible realized Sweaty was mocking him for the way he'd greeted Sweaty when he'd gotten out of the hole. The two embraced with a handshake and a quick hug.

Chapter 16

Ain't No Friends In This Shit

"My nigga, what the fuck?!" Possible asked.

"Bro, they was tryna give me a program for that shit, but headquarters shot it down," Sweaty declared with a huge smile. "I thought I was cooked. They said D-man flat lined twice. I Like It Here got fifteen years for that," Sweaty explained.

"That shit was crazy. I caught the end of it," Possible said.

"Look, I knew somethin was funny when he said he wasn't gonna see Zay for a minute," Sweaty said, going through his brown paper bag looking for his hygiene.

"Ay, my nigga, throw all that shit away and grab the new stuff up on the shelf. Lemme get out your way," Possible said, giving Sweaty room to get himself situated.

"I was hot, thinkin 'Of all the damn days, it had to be on the day of the drop.' I just knew headquarters was signin off on the program. I thought, 'by the time I get out, niggas will be gone to mediums and shit.'"

While Sweaty washed his face and armpits, he vented with his back to Possible who seized the perfect moment to pull out a fat stick and set it on the desk without a word.

"My nigga, I'm tellin you I was trippin. I thought it was over." Sweaty said, drying his face and turning to look at Possible, who had a sly grin on his face.

"Why you smilin like that?" Sweaty asked.

"I'm just happy my nigga's back. What, I can't smile now?" Possible exclaimed.

"Naw, you look real shady right now," Sweaty said. His eyes began to wander around the cell, and the moment he caught the stick lying on the desk, the same sly grin lit up his face.

"They bout to do count right now," Possible said.

"They walkin right now," Sweaty replied, peeking out the cell window.

"Bro they had me in the back beefin!"

"Who?" Possible asked.

"Sergeant Jackson, talkin bout they don't want no problems, and if anything happens, no matter how small, they gonna put me *under* the hole," Sweaty said, smiling.

"That's crazy!"

"Mr. Washington, welcome back, we almost lost you," CO Peters said as he walked by doing count.

CO Peters, walking behind Peters, added "They sent your property to long-term storage. I called for it already, so maybe tomorrow."

Sweaty and Possible were so excited that they didn't realize the stick wasn't covered up. The two officers could sense they were up to no good. Possible heard Peters make a comment about them to Peters.

"Two peas in a pod," Peters replied.

"Grab the lighter and let's get it," Sweaty snapped.

"Ay, cover the…" Possible said, pointing to the cell speaker. Sweaty grabbed a tissue, dampened it, and proceeded to cover the speaker.

"While we blowin, Ima bring you up to date on everythin," Possible said, pulling out his own stick. The two sparked, and Possible began to update Sweaty on the order of the operation.

"I was hearin bout you niggas in the hole too—y'all got it poppin," Sweaty said.

"What did I tell you from the jump? Help me and I got you," Possible said, exhaling a cloud of smoke.

Sweaty smiled, feeling the smoke and the camaraderie between the two.

"We bout to pick up any day now, too, so just keep low-key and let's get this money," Possible said excitedly.

"I'm already knowin baby supposed to be comin up too. I need to shoot her a couple bucks for gas and shit," Sweaty said.

"Don't even trip, just let me know how much," Possible replied. "Here, this is all you right here," he added, handing Sweaty about a cap and a half of smoke. "Just joog it and use the money for that."

"Good lookin," Sweaty replied. The two finished their sticks and began to scheme on the moves Sweaty had come up with while in the hole. They stayed up really late, going over different ways to make money, gossiping, and discussing the latest dramas. They felt a little sluggish as they got ready for breakfast. The two men couldn't remember the walk to the chow hall.

"What's up my nigga? When'd you get out? They said you was gettin a program." Zay greeted Sweaty with the City handshake, then shook Possible's hand before joining them at the table. "You niggas look burnt out," he said.

"Man, we just went to sleep a few hours ago," Possible said.

"Ay, I'm just bout done wit that pack too."

"Did you use the money app?" Possible asked.

"Just like you told me," Zay answered.

"Where my ten bucks?" Possible asked. Zay just smiled and pulled out two meat sticks and a packet of beef crumbles.

Possible counted the value of each item as it was handed to him. "Two dollars... four dollars... seven dollars—you three bucks short, my nigga."

"I couldn't bring everythin. Don't trip, I got you," Zay replied.

"You just now payin that ten?" Sweaty asked.

"You niggas gonna stop houndin me over pennies? I'm sendin paperbacks," Zay snapped.

"What's good?" Zay asked Sweaty. "You straight? Need anythin? You get your property yet?"

"I should get my shit today," Sweaty answered.

"Did you put the kite in to move over like we talked bout?" Possible asked Zay.

"I kept forgettin," Zay shot back.

"He was supposed to move in wit me," Possible said to Sweaty.

"Change of plans. That ain't gonna work," Sweaty said.

"I don't see any more food on those trays, gentlemen," a CO announced as he walked by.

"Where Matt at?" Zay asked as the three proceeded to tray up and leave the chow hall.

"At work. You know he got that kitchen job now," Possible answered.

"Yeah, I see y'all puttin it together."

"We got this other move, too. That's why we need you over here," Sweaty said, as the three hit the breezeway.

"Noticing CO Hunter, Possible yelled, "Ms. Hunter, haven't seen you in a while."

"Vacation," Hunter replied. "I heard y'all been misbehaving, Mr. Washington."

"Fake news!" Sweaty yelled, as the men reached the main entrance to their unit.

"Aight, bro, in a minute," Sweaty said to Zay as the two shook hands.

"Aight, bro," Zay said to Possible as they shook hands.

"Put this nigga on already," Zay said to Sweaty, meaning allow Possible to be from City G's.

"Fuck you mean?" I'm puttin *you* on, Possible replied half-jokingly. Possible and Sweaty made it back to the cell only to be pulled out ten minutes later.

"Jenkins! Washington!" the booth officer ordered through the cell intercom. "To the holding cell please."

"What the fuck?" Possible uttered under his breath.

"Aw, shit!" Sweaty said. The two looked at each other and headed to the holding cell.

The booth officer directed them over the hall speaker: "Jenkins, please step into holding cell 1. Washington into cell 2, please."

"Look, man, I told Sergeant Jackson ain't gonna be no problems," Sweaty said, as he entered holding cell #2. Two minutes later CO Vasquez arrived.

"All right, I need you to strip down and hand me everything through the cuff board," Vasquez ordered.

"Vasquez, what's goin on?" Possible asked as he removed his clothes.

"This has nothing to do with us in the unit. It came from higher up, that's all I can tell you," Vasquez answered as he searched each piece of clothing they handed him.

"All right," Vasquez said to Possible, "mouth, ears, armpits, lift, separate. Okay, turn around, show me the bottoms of your feet, bend and spread. Okay, get dressed."

While Sweaty was put through the strip procedure, Possible's heart began to race. He knew Sweaty had smoke on him.

"All right, turn around, show me the bottoms of your feet, bend and spread. Okay, get dressed," Vasquez said.

Hearing the words "get dressed" was a huge relief for Possible.

"All right gentlemen, hang tight. We're gonna conduct a cell search. We'll be as quick as possible," said Vasquez, walking off. The two men sat while their cell was searched. Possible began to wonder if anything would be out of place. He formed a mental picture of the cell, trying to remember what it had looked like before they went to chow. Once again, Possible's heart began to race. They'd both been up so late that his mental picture was foggy due to lack of sleep.

"Ay, bro!" Possible said in a loud whisper.

"Yeah," Sweaty answered.

"Bro, we dint leave any appliances on, did we?" Possible asked, speaking in code.

"I turned everythin off 'fore we went to breakfast," Sweaty answered. Possible began to relax, and wondered what had brought this about. He heard CO Vasquez's voice in his head: *This has nothing to do with us in the unit. It came from higher up.*

Although this was Possible's first bid, he knew that "higher up" was not good. This would be the topic of discussion in the next yard he got with Matt and Sweaty. After Possible and Sweaty had sat in the holding cells for almost an hour, CO Vasquez and two other COs came back to talk to them about their cell search.

"All right, gentlemen, you guys keep a clean cell, and we tried to keep it clean as possible," one CO said. "We left a search report. We only took a few miscellaneous things, a couple items with the wrong DOC numbers on them—no biggie, we didn't write any infraction.

"Not this time," CO Vasquez teased.

Possible and Sweaty headed back to their cell. On the way, Possible just couldn't wait to ask, "My nigga, where the smoke at?"

"I got it on me," Sweaty whispered.

"He didn't see it when you spread?" Possible asked.

"You spread?" Sweaty asked, shocked. Embarrassed, Possible became quiet. He hate getting strip-searched, hated to think of all the times he'd been asked to bend over and spread.

"You *never* spread," Sweaty replied. "I never had a guard say, 'Hey you didn't spread.' Just think how that would sound coming out his mouth. They hate it just as much as we do, most of 'em, anyway."

The two walked into their cell and found it not too messy. It could have been a lot worse, but an untidy cell was far from Possible's mind. Recalling the "higher up" remark made by CO Vasquez, it dawned on Possible that Vasquez had been referring to Administration Frazier!

"Man, would you stop pacin and sit down?" Sweaty said. "It's been two days since the cell search and it's been all bad since then."

"My nigga, you heard Matt: Frazier is on Dam'on. It all makes sense; that's why they hit us like that, and why the drop ain't come yet," Possible said.

"Look, Matt just tryna take the heat off hisself. The nigga in the kitchen that got cracked prob'ly got the shit from Matt, that's why we got hit like that. Think bout it—why would they hit us and Matt but not Dam'on?" Sweaty said as he rolled a stick.

"You ask me, we got to watch Matt. Get the lighter ready," Sweaty said.

"You just don't give a fuck, sitting there rollin while they out there plottin, prob'ly waitin on you to spark that," Possible snapped.

"If they comin, at least we'll be keed. You rather be in the hole sober?" Sweaty asked.

"I rather not be in the hole at all," Possible shot back. "Tell me this, then, why the drop ain't come, huh? Why the dog been in Pod 3 the last two days?"

"I can tell you this: Dam'on seen that dog and ain't nothin drippin or droppin," Sweaty said. "We bout to smoke, so you can calm down. Then when we go to yard we can all have a big powwow."

"Remember when CO Vasquez said the search came from higher up?" Possible asked.

"No, but I remember I told you to get the lighter ready," Sweaty replied.

"My nigga, aight, we'll see," a frustrated Possible said as he put the lighter together.

"Don't overreact to these strip searches and dogs and shit; we in prison, that's what they do, searches, and bring dogs around to try and find the smoke. Long as they don't catch you wit it, it's all good," Sweaty said, the stick hanging from his lips, waiting to be lit.

"I hear what you sayin, it's just Matt looked spooked. The drop was supposed to be yesterday or day before. Dogs all in Pod 3 where Dam'on lives, that's fishy," Possible said.

"It might be, but we can't stop it, so let's blow now in case they on the way," Sweaty said.

Possible sparked the stick, and they began to get keed.

"We bout to go to yard and figure everythin out. Don't trip." Sweaty inhaled a cloud of smoke before passing the stick to Possible, who smoked, deep in thought, as Sweaty went over different scenarios.

"Dam'on works in laundry. The kitchen I saw holds another buildin, so for Matt to put that on Dam'on ain't addin up. He said he got cracked with three caps, right?"

"Yeah, somethin like that," Possible said, passing the stick in a trance-like state.

"How he know, unless the nigga told him he got it from Dam'on, but we bout to see Dam'on in a minute." Sweaty was trying to get Possible to see that things would get figured out.

"What we need to figure out is this move I been tellin you bout wit the white boy. We make that happen, we ain't gotta worry if Dam'on hot or not," Sweaty said.

This jolted Possible out of his trance. "My nigga, this ain't bout the move or Dam'on bein hot; this bout niggas' livelihood. I told you how much was ridin on this and how my family is hurtin. How you and Dam'on ain't in the same spot. You think niggas is out here doin this shit cause they like?" Possible spoke more aggressively than Sweaty had ever heard him do.

"Look, you care too much." Sweaty raised his own aggression to a higher level, then took a hard hit off the stick before passing it. "You think Dam'on gives a fuck bout you or your family? Don't get this shit twisted, mothafuckas all family and close and shit. This is prison. Niggas don't give a fuck bout you. Do something to fuck wit his bread or get in his way, you'll see a whole different person. Better get your feelins outta this shit and keep your head in it. The minute you get caught thinkin these niggas is your friends is the minute you become a liability. Ain't no friends in this shit, just niggas pretendin to be!

"You got a good heart, Possible. You come from a good family. I seen that in you when we first met. You got that type of aura that'll get you far in the free world, but it could cost you in here."

Possible just listened while he killed the stick and flushed the roach. He could understand exactly where Sweaty was coming from, because it sounded like Charlie talking to him.

"H Unit, prepare for yard! H Unit Yard!"

On the way there, Possible, Sweaty, and Matt walked in silence, each feeling the tension among them—one hoping not to be exposed and the other two looking for answers. The three entered the yard on a mission.

"What's up, my nigga?" Zay greeted Sweaty.

"Ay," Sweaty said to Possible and Matt, "Ima go fuck wit my niggas real quick. I'll be back." He and Zay walked off toward the group of City G's.

"There go Dam'on ova there!" Matt announced, breaking the awkward silence between the two.

"Yeah, I see 'im. Ima wait a li'l bit before I go talk to 'im," Possible said.

"Make sure you find out what happen wit the boy in the kitchen."

"What was his name again?" Possible asked.

"Reggie."

"That's what he go by, Reggie?"

"Yep." Dam'on know who he is, he old-school, he been down since the early nineties," Matt replied.

"Here he come now," Possible said, seeing Dam'on walking toward him. "Aight, I'll be back."

"Yep. I'm bout to use the phone," Matt shot back.

"What's good, bro!" Possible asked as the two men shook hands with an embrace.

"You tell me, y'all got it poppin, Dam'on replied, smiling.

"I was trippin, expectin the drop, but me and my cellie got ambushed by outside COs, strip-searched, all the shit and stuffses, then Matt gets off work they hit him too, he dint even make it to the cell. And the dog in your Pod—I'm trippin."

"That's why I dint shoot. It's crazy, I was puttin it together when the dog was in the unit, so I was like, naw, don't push, just be patient, it be like that sometimes."

"They always bring the dog back to back like that?" Possible asked.

"They do what they wanna do. It could be the native guy gettin popped in the kitchen holdin shit, that's why it's so hot," Dam'on explained.

"That's your guy?"

"Naw, my guy standin over there. I fucked wit him before, but that wasn't my shit. I thought that was y'all. That's why y'all got hit like that," Dam'on said. Possible took a second to process the information.

"Y'all straight, right?" Dam'on asked.

"Yeah, we good, but while we was getting' hit, CO Vasquez said it's from higher up."

"Higher up!" Dam'on snapped.

"That's what I said. This nigga thinkin it's the norm, but the way he said, like he dint wanna be doin the search, it was forced," Possible said.

"Never go against your gut. If you wanna press pause, press pause."

"I dint think it was me, I thought it was you," Possible replied.

"Me? Naw, ain't no change wit my environment. I pay attention to detail. Like I told you, you'll see it before it comes."

Hearing Dam'on say these words made Possible's stomach turn.

"You think it's me?" Possible asked.

"The boy went to the hole from the kitchen. They searched you guys, nothin was found… that could be end of that. Anything else happen since then?"

"Naw, everythin went back to normal," Possible said.

"So what's the move? You want me to put it together?" Dam'on asked.

After some thought Possible's gut was telling him to just chill and wait, but he had a few [joogs] who had preordered, and because the drop was already behind, he didn't wanna keep them waiting. He hated preorders because they became obligations, and Possible hated obligations.

"Fuck it, we good, Shoot it."

"You sure? Better safe than sorry."

"Naw, I got people been waitin. They already shot the cake and everythin," Possible said.

"So tomorrow. You know the drill," Dam'on said, shaking Possible's hand and walking back to his group

Possible now had more questions now than he'd had before meeting with Dam'on. Matt's story wasn't adding up.

"What's up?" Matt asked. "What he say?"

"He said he thought it was us."

"That wasn't his pack Reggie got caught with?" Matt asked.

"Dam'on said he fucked wit him before, but that wasn't his pack," Possible said.

"One of them niggas lyin!" Matt snapped. "What he say bout the drop?"

"We good tomorrow." Possible answered.

"Tomorrow. For sure?" Matt asked eagerly.

"Yeah, but I dunno if I wanna bust down," Possible replied, suspicious.

"Look, do what you want, but I got bread on the line, so let me know."

"Yeah, I know. I got bread on the line too. It's just this higher-up shit fuckin wit me," Possible said.

"If Dam'on coo wit shootin you the pack, then trust and believe it's good."

"Yeah, I know that's what he was sayin: cause they dint find nothin, it's over wit."

"That's what I been tellin you, you thinkin too hard. Let's get this paper!" Matt yelled.

Possible felt a little better after talking to Dam'on. *If he ain't trippin, why should I be trippin?* Possible had been making moves long enough to know that the law don't want small fry, they want the big fish!

Chapter 17

Ain't Adding Up

Early next morning, the day of the drop, Possible tossed and turned, unable to sleep. He got up to piss and could hear Sweaty snoring. After he washed his hands he peeked out the cell window to check the unit clock, which read 4:30 a.m. *Two hours till morning count,* he thought. With no choice but to climb back into his bunk, Possible lay on his back, eyes open, thinking about everything that has happened the past several months. The stabbing, the Forbidden 3, strip-searches, the kitchen ordeal. *Okay, I had nothin to do wit the stabbin, but havin the smoke on me when the guards put me on Forbidden 3—just imagine if they told me to spread.* Then the kitchen ordeal wit Matt. What if their spot got compromised, and Matt didn't know it? The dogs in the unit for two days straight, but nothin found; Sweaty had smoke on him, strip-searched and nothin found. While everybody else was celebratin, claimin victory by grabbin another pack, Possible wasn't so sure he was ready to do his victory dance. *I got to tighten this up, there's no more room for error,* he thought. If they'd ever been, the odds were no longer in his favor. He closed his eyes, no more thoughts, not even the sound of Sweaty's snoring.

* * *

"Dam'on said that wasn't his pack, right?" Sweaty asked.

"Yep."

"And now Matt talkin bout somebody lyin… yeah, somebody is *you!*" Sweaty snapped, then put a big scoop of oatmeal in his mouth.

"Yeah, but how we know Dam'on ain't lyin?" Possible asked, pouring syrup on his pancakes.

"What would Dam'on have to lie for?"

"So we can keep pickin up from him."

"You do got a point there. Don't wanna get your clientele spooked, that'll dry up the bread. So what did Matt say when you told 'im Dam'on said it wasn't his pack?"

"I told you, he said one of 'em lyin!" Possible replied.

"Look, it don't matter. I told you we got this other avenue, and we can put Dam'on out. It's a win-win." Sweaty said, finishing his oatmeal.

"I hear you. I'm supposed to be pickin up today, anytime, so we'll see what's up," Possible said casually.

"Ay, top of the mornin!" Zay said, sitting down at the table with Sweaty and Possible. "So did y'all figure it out? I put the kite to come over too," he told them.

"That's what's up. We gotta find you a cell," Sweaty replied.

"Oh, you ain't comin out the cell to fuck wit me?"

"And leave Possible stuck wit some weirdo?" Sweaty said.

"It's coo," Possible said. "I'll just move to a single cell."

"Look, we'll figure all that out when you get over here," Sweaty replied. "You ain't gonna eat that oatmeal?" he asked, eyeing Possible's tray.

"Go 'head," Possible said.

"So are we on, or what?" Sweaty asked.

"Oh, Dam'on told me to tell you, it's this mornin," Zay said.

"That's all he said was 'this mornin?" Possible asked.

"Shit, I know what it means," Sweaty said with a smile.

"Yeah. Don't trip, we got yard this afternoon," Possible replied.

"Same thing?" Zay asked.

"Same thing."

"I'm bout to put all the bread on my Jpay this time," Zay said with a smile.

"Y'all ready?" Possible asked. "I got shit to do."

"Yeah, come on. Don't let me be the reason," Sweaty replied.

"I ain't all that hungry no more, anyway," Zay added.

They trayed up and walked out of the chow hall all smiles, happy and excited.

"Come here, Jenkins," CO Hunter ordered, grinning. "Stand for search! Washington and Grant, keep it moving."

"How you doin today?" Possible asked as he assumed the position for a pat search.

"I'm doing much better now," Hunter whispered in Possible's ear as she began to rub him down in a seductive way. It was a natural reaction. Possible dropped his hands and started to turn to see if it was really her.

"Continue to stand for search, Mr. Jenkins!" Hunter ordered, stopping Possible from facing her.

"I could get used to this," Possible whispered.

"Well, we'll see. I start working in H-unit next week. Have a nice day," Hunter said, as she slid her hands across Possible's butt.

Possible had to walk fast to the unit; he didn't want people to notice his dick was hard. He quickly took his thoughts elsewhere before entering the unit. Sweaty and Zay were right there to greet him.

"What was all that bout?" Sweaty asked.

"Mac player. I see you," Zay said. "What she say?"

"Nothin!" Possible answered.

"She said somethin," Sweaty teased.

"She asked me… how many apples I took from the chow hall."

"Yeah, whatever," Zay said.

The CO booth officer ordered: "Keep it moving, gentlemen!"

"Aight, bro, go to yard," Zay said.

"Let's go to the gym. I'm tryna hoop," Sweaty replied.

"Aight, I'll see y'all at the gym."

Possible was in another world. He'd never felt like this in his life. The feeling was unfamiliar, a mix of excitement, butterflies, uncertain'ty that what had just happened was real. *Was Hunter playin some type of sick game?* Possible was so deep in his thoughts that by the time he surfaced he was already in his cell and Sweaty was asking him about the drop, which he'd forgotten all about.

"Bro, you not even listenin to me."

"Yeah, I heard you. We goin to the gym," Possible replied, snapping back to reality.

"I ought to kick you in your motherfuckin head. Ain't nobody say nothin bout no gym," Sweaty said playfully.

"What you say?" Possible asked.

"I said how in the hell you gonna get the drop and there's no movement.

Possible jumped up from his bunk to look out the cell door. He could see no movement, no dayroom, no unit workers, no laundry bags, as if the unit were on lockdown.

"Ay, Vasquez, what's goin on?" Sweaty asked, as Vasquez did a tier check.

"We are on restricted movement," said Vasquez.

"We not havin dayroom or yard?" Sweaty asked.

"Nope. No outside movement."

"What happened?" Possible asked, moving Sweaty away from the cell window.

"I don't know. This came from higher up," Vasquez replied, walking away.

Possible's head began to spin and he suddenly felt nauseous.

"That's fucked up. I really wanted to hoop, too," Sweaty said. "What's wrong wit you?"

"Dam'on!" Possible answered, staring blankly.

"Dam'on? What bout Da—oh, shit!" Sweaty blurted.

"I knew something funny was goin on. I just knew it!" Possible snapped.

"It could be a fight or staff accountability," Sweaty suggested. "Come on, they just walked. Let's blow, and by the time we done we'll know what's up."

Sweaty pulled out the last of the smoke. Possible started to prepare the lighter while Sweaty tried to roll.

"Ay, you gotta do this, my hands are sweaty," he said.

They switched tasks without a word.

"Don't trip, my nigga," Sweaty said. "Everythin gonna be aight. You gotta think positive, it's the law of attraction."

"Matt was right this whole time, and we dint believe 'im," Possible said.

"Who dint believe 'im? All I said was we gotta watch Matt. I dint say he was lyin."

Possible just gave Sweaty the *I know you dint say that* look.

"Or did I?" Sweaty added, feeling guilty under Possible's stare.

Possible put the stick to his lips, and Sweaty lit it. Possible took a deep pull, then passed it to Sweaty.

"CO Vasquez said restricted movement, not lockdown. That means it's serious, but not that serious," Possible said.

"Did you already pay for the drop?" Sweaty asked.

"Naw, I don't think so. I told baby I would call today."

"I know you glad you dint."

"What happed to the positive law of attraction shit? We don't know for sure."

"Possible!... Possible!... Possible!"

Possible jumped of the bunk, and passed Sweaty the stick. Looking out the cell window, he saw Matt, off from work early, walking back to his cell.

"I told you!" Matt yelled. "They just wrapped up Dam'on, J-money, Li'l D, Shmoney—damn near all the Burgundy B's."

"What happened?" Possible asked, worried.

"I dunno, but they got the laundry room roped off like a crime scene," Matt said.

"No!" Possible yelled.

"Yep. They sendin workers back one by one from the kitchen and laundry," Matt said as he stepped into his cell.

This made Possible paranoid.

"Oh, shit, you think they comin to get us?" he asked Sweaty, who was still puffing on the stick.

"Here, kill this. I know how you can get." Sweaty said, handing Possible the end of the stick. Possible took the last couple drags and flushed the roach.

"They wrapped them niggas up cause they knew they was part of the operation," Sweaty said

"That's what I'm talkin bout. We had our own operation goin on," Possible said, pacing back and forth.

"Yeah, but notice those were all his boys, and if they wanted you they woulda got you by now," Sweaty said, trying to calm Possible down.

The booth officer announced: "Attention H-unit. After shift change the unit will resume normal movement!"

"Well, that's that!" Sweaty said.

The announcement relaxed Possible a bit, but he was still shaken up because he didn't know the extent of the Dam'on situation. For now he would remain low-key and see what developed.

Chapter 18

The Fall

Later that day Possible, Sweaty, Matt, and two other inmates were in the dayroom playing poker and gossiping about the latest events.

"Aight, gentlemen, Omaha wit a bonus must play two," Matt said, dealing the cards.

"Who all did they snatch up?" Sweaty asked, putting his poker hand together.

"Damn near all the Burgundy B's," Matt replied.

"Five hundred to see the flop!" Possible said.

"Call!"

"Call!"

"Call!"

"Call!"

"Everybody called?" Matt asked before he flipped over the first three cards.

"How much work did they find?" Possible asked, checking his hand.

"Shit, I dint see everythin, but I seen bags bein carried out of a li'l hole behind the big-ass dryers," one of the poker players who worked in laundry said.

"Bags?" Sweaty asked, betting another $500 to see the turn card.

"Call!"

"Call!"

"Call!"

"Dam'on won't be back for a minute, Raise to $1,500," Possible said, shaking his head in disbelief.

"Call!"

"Fold!"

"Fold!"

"Fold!"

"Johnny, you don't ever fold," Matt said, while folding his own hand.

"You know what they say bout us Asians—we bold, we don't fold, now show me the gold!"

As they waited for the turn card, Matt took a second and flipped the card. It paired the board.

"Check!" To da man wit da plan," Johnny freestyled again.

"What I got left, Matt?" Possible asked looking at the chip count being kept on paper.

"You got five thousand left!" Matt answered.

"Five thousand!" Possible yelled.

"Call!" Johnny snapped, turning over four of a kind and dancing at the same time.

"Damn, I got the biggest boat too," Possible said, slapping his cards on the table.

"Yeah, I knew you had boat!" Johnny said, still dancing.

"You want another buy-in?" Matt asked.

"Naw, I'm bout to see what's up wit the phone," Possible said.

"Don't trip, cellie, I'm bout to crack 'em," Sweaty announced as Possible left the table. Possible still felt a little down about the Dam'on situation, not just because he wasn't getting the drop but because he actually felt bad for Dam'on. Possible looked up to him, he was a coo guy, and Possible hated seeing bad things happen to good people. He knew just the person to call to cheer him up.

"Hello, GG."

"Hey, baby! You sound down. What's wrong?" GG asked.

"They canceled yard today, we been stuck in the cell all day, that's all."

"Well, you never could lie very good, but Ima tell you somethin: they can keep your body captive, but once you let them capture your mind, that's when they got you. You remember what Grandma taught you?"

"I do: Always remember, through Jesus Christ we can do all things."

"That's right. In unison, GG and Possible intoned: "Once he opens a door, can't no man close it; once he closes a door, can't no man open it."

GG could hear Possible smiling from ear to ear now.

"No man or thing can have dominion over us, unless we allow it to. You can't let your outside dictate how you feel on the inside, but let your inside, your spirt, dictate your outside, and these small things won't bother you. You got a good spirit, Pierre, don't let them take that away, you hear me?"

"Yes, ma'am. You told me you was gonna let me hear the song next time I call," Possible reminded her.

"What song?" GG joked.

"Naw, you ain't gonna play that one on me."

"Ha-ha-ha!" GG Burst out laughing.

Her laughter was contagious. If GG started laughing, Possible laughed just as hard.

"What you say, boy, you ain't foolin me wit that one!" GG was laughing so hard she was barely able to finish her sentence.

"Ha-ha-ha! Talkin bout what song," Possible replied, trying to regain his composure. "All of a sudden tryna play the memory-loss game. Naw."

"Whew! Aight let me get it real quick," GG replied.

"See, there you go again. You ain't gotta get it, you know it by heart."

This made GG laugh so hard she started to cry, choke, and cough at the same time.

"Boy, you better stop if you wanna hear this song! Oh, my stomach!."

"Aight, Ima let you get it together," Possible replied.

"Aight. It's been a minute since you called, so I been working on other songs too, but I got it now, hold up."

GG sipped some water, cleared her throat, and proceeded to sing:

"I've been traveling / for some time / far, far away / On that old dusty road / so I don't know / when I'll be home / So pray for me / pray for me / I need you to pray for me / while you wait for me."

Possible got lost in GG's voice, she got one of those old down-south voices, the negro spirituals type voice.

"You repeat that three times. I'm thinking of adding some more. What you think?"

"I think that's filthy, GG," Possible said.

"Boy, I thought you was gonna say 'tight,'" GG replied.

"We don't say tight no more, GG. It's played out," Possible explained.

"So filthy is the new tight?"

"Yes, ma'am."

"You have sixty seconds remaining!"

"Aight, GG. I love you, and Ima call again soon."

"Thirty seconds remaining."

"Aight, baby, I love you too, and don't wait so long to call."

"I won't."

"Bye, baby."

Possible hung up the phone feeling good again. *Works every time*, he thought, as he made his way to the Jpay kiosk. Sitting down at the kiosk, Possible saw that he had no new messages. This was shocking, since there had never been a time when there was no messages.

"Who's up on the table?" Possible yelled across the dayroom.

"I told you I got you!" Sweaty yelled back.

Surprised by the response, Possible went to check it out for himself.

"Twenty-five hundred to see the flop!" Sweaty announced.

"Call!"

"Call!"

"That's my all in," Brandon announced as he called.

"It's getting' real over here—twenty-five hundred just to see the flop," Possible said, feeling the intensity.

"Ay, Possible, can I talk to you a minute?" an inmate asked.

They stepped away from the table where they could have a bit more privacy.

"What's good?" Possible asked.

"Ay, my name is Crazy. The homie Joker wanted me to ask if you could hook him up at yard tomorrow."

"Naw, ain't nothin poppin. It's over. Tell Joker I holla at 'im at yard," Possible replied, feeling a bit uneasy about the conversation.

"Aight, homie, I'll let him know," Crazy said as he walked away.

Possible thought: *How do the biggest bust in prison history happen, and hours later people wanna try and make moves?* He realized there was going to be a major drought, a money pit that he could capitalize on if he wanted to. *If there ever was an opportunity, now's the time. I'll just be in and out, stack enough money where the family be straight, and be done.* Possible could hear Charlie's voice, which had now become his own voice: "We do this cause we have to, not cause we want to. When our paper is right, then we do what we want to."

Possible had enough experience now to be able to hit and run. "All I need's bout ten, fifteen bands," he whispered to himself. "It's definitely doable." Just with this short run he'd been on, he'd already touched close to five bands. He would simply have to learn from Dam'on's mistakes and make sure his team stayed on point. "All the *i*'s dotted and *t*'s crossed. Keep it simple," Possible whispered. The only problem was that he had to find another way in, no more Dam'on. Then it clicked.

"Ay, Sweaty!"

The booth officer announced: "Dayroom is closed! Cell in. Dayroom is over!"

Chapter 19

The Rise

It had been nearly two months since the fall of Dam'on and the Burgundy B's. To say there was a drought would be an understatement. What was once two or three bucks for a stick was now ten bucks. A cap, if you could find one, now cost $300, and anything over that, forget about it!

As he grabbed his dinner tray, Possible apologized: "Matt, let me be the first to say, 'my bad' for doubtin you when you tried to tell us bout Dam'on bein hot."

"I was tryna tell him you know your shit," Sweaty said.

"Look, I was just tryna get y'all to understand that it was time to switch it up," Matt replied as the three of them took their seats.

"Now look: ten bucks for a stick and we sittin round here broke and sober," Matt lamented as he took a bite of his hotdog.

"I know," Sweaty replied. "I had to buy four just to get 'em for five bucks apiece."

"You got smoke?" Possible asked.

"You *know* he got smoke. See, there y'all go playin them games. I thought we was all in this together," Matt said, feeling left out of the loop.

"Don't y'all still owe a few bucks from the last run?" Possible shot back.

"Shit, we bout even if we keepin score."

"Even!" Possible retorted.

"Yeah. How many times I cut you a deal on the poker table?" Matt asked.

"Oh, I thought we was in this shit together?" Possible mocked.

"So I take it we gonna fuck wit the white boy who got the move, right?" Sweaty asked, taking a bite of mac 'n' cheese.

"Who, the white boy?" Matt asked.

"Jessie," Sweaty said.

"The one that works as a groundskeeper?" Matt asked.

"Yeah. He got the move where baby make the drop and he brings it to us," Sweaty said.

"How much at a time?"

"No more than a zip if it's packed right, but we can hit three times a week."

"What he wants?" Possible asked.

"For every twenty-eight G's he wants seven."

"If he got the move, then why he need us?" Matt asked.

"That what I said," Possible interjected, finishing his second hotdog.

"He don't got nobody to make the drop."

"What bout his people?"

"See, that's the thing. He don't want them to know cause they could make it hot and cut him out the deal," Sweaty said.

"I know who you talkin bout, too" said Matt. "He don't really fuck wit dem guys like that either."

"That's tricky, cause it could start a problem if they find out," Possible said.

"Yeah—a problem for *him*," Matt snapped. "Who we gonna have makin the drop?" he asked Sweaty.

"Me and Possible gonna take turns."

"I told you I wasn't a hundred percent if baby was gonna be good wit it," Possible said.

"It's good either way. Zay gets visits too, and he bout to move over here," Sweaty said.

"Where is Zay?" Possible asked.

"At a visit." Sweaty replied. "I already talked to him; he probably givin her the play now."

"Aight, you know we still got the spot in the kitchen, too, so let's make it happen," Matt said.

"Look, we gotta be on point. You know they waitin on somebody to take Dam'on spot," Possible replied.

"There's no reason why we should be caught wit anythin, just keep everythin put up," Matt said.

"Aight, Ima tell baby to slide through on the next visit and we'll see what's up," Possible said.

"Mines already comin," Sweaty said.

"And Ima make sure the spot still good," Matt added.

All in agreement now, the three proceeded to tray up. On the way back to the unit, it dawned on Possible: "Matt, we dint have no smoke left when all that Dam'on shit happen?"

"When I got back from work, I gave you bout a quarter cap when we had dayroom, and I told you I kept a li'l less than a quarter cap."

"I don't remember that," Sweaty said.

"That's what I'm sayin," Possible said.

"If there was anything left it was crumbs," Matt said.

Possible made a mental note to make sure he kept count. They entered the unit feeling motivated. Now was the perfect time to capitalize on the fact that Dam'on was gone and the market was in flux. They could continue to charge high-end prices till someone else came along and tried to undercut their prices, in which case they'd be prepared to go as low need be.

For the past couple weeks, Possible's morning schedule had changed, and Sweaty had noticed.

"Damn you up before me again. Don't think I'm not payin attention," Sweaty said as he jumped off the top bunk.

"Yeah, this is the new and improved me," Possible declared, rolling a stick.

"Oh, yeah? And just how are you improved?"

"Well, since you been payin attention, you know we been doin really well, so it got me feelin like we runnin a corporation," Possible said.

"You sure it's not CO Hunter workin in the unit the last couple of weeks?" Sweaty asked as he put the lighter together.

Possible just smiled because he knew Sweaty was right. In addition to making a lot money, Possible had been living on top of the world. The operation was going just as planned, and CO Hunter's working in the unit had been a bonus.

"My turn to first toke," Sweaty ordered, sparking the stick.

"I can do that, since I'm in a good mood," Possible replied.

"So I talked to Jessie and he's ready for another drop."

"Already? We still got the pack from the other day, haven't even touched it," Possible said, passing the stick.

"I know. I'm just lettin you know so we can always be on deck," Sweaty replied, inhaling smoke.

"Aight, look, we got bout $4,000 to collect. Let's get the majority of that, then we put more merchandise on the market," Possible said. He believed they should run their business like a legit enterprise and use legit language, though their biz was the furthest thing from legitimate.

"That make sense. I'll have everythin ready to go by then," Sweaty replied, flushing the last of the stick.

Possible sat back, earbuds in, listening to his oldies playlist, which included Bobby Womack, Rick James, Bootsy Collins, and Teddy Pendergrass. With ten bands in the bank and another four to be collected, and still holding product waiting to hit the market, he had no worries, no stress, and most important, no competition. *What would Charlie think if he knew the money he been gettin from Sabrina was actually comin from me?* An operation

Possible himself was running, the guy who called the plays. This was Possible making a way, so Charlie couldn't be upset. On the yard later that day, Possible, Sweaty, Matt, and Zay were going over business.

"Like I was sayin, lets collect that four bands fore we put out any more product," Possible told the other three.

"I hear you, but I got a few people wantin to shoot cake now," Zay said.

"How much?" Possible asked.

"Shit, altogether bout $800 right now!" Zay answered.

"When you gonna get that?" Sweaty asked.

"Look, everythin put up. I don't go back to work for another two days," Matt replied.

"That's perfect then. We should be closer to collectin. My joog said his bread gonna hit in three days. That's damn near half the four bands," Sweaty said.

"Zay, tell your joog to shoot it, and when it clears you'll shoot it to 'im. Sweaty, let Jessie know we ready for another drop, and tell Joker it's good and see if he's ready for another one," Possible said.

"What bout Brandon?" Matt asked.

"Oh, yeah, you give 'im half now and the other half when his bread clears. I'm not too worried bout Brandon; he's in our pod and his bread is good," Possible said.

"When will the drop be, so I can have my people ready?" Matt asked.

"The next visit." As the words were rolling off Possible's tongue, he felt uncomfortable. Even though Matt was on his team, his and Sweaty's number-one rule was never reveal times and dates to anyone.

"*Maybe* the next visit," Sweaty quickly added, trying to cover Possible's mistake without making it too obvious.

"Y'all just let me know. I'm in the pod now," Zay said.

"Hopefully I can live by myself. I don't want no cellie," Zay told the other men.

"You good. They ain't gonna put just anybody in your cell," Sweaty replied.

"Aight, we all on the same page. Everybody good?" Possible asked.

"Yep," Matt answered as Sweaty and Zay nodded their heads in agreement.

"I'm bout to use the phone," Possible said, walking off. On his way, he was stopped by four different inmates he'd never met before, all asking to spend money, and all four times he pretended to know nothing. A smile formed on Possible's face as he dialed Charlie's number. He was no longer in Charlie's shadow, he was his own man, running his own operation, answering to nobody, the feeling of being a somebody that everyone knows. He thought about telling Charlie.

Charlie answered the phone. "Peety! bout time you hit a nigga."

"I know. A lot been goin on," Possible replied.

"Ain't that much goin on in the world that I can't get a few minutes of your time. I been locked up, so I know how it gets, but it's unacceptable. I thought we already had this conversation."

"I know." Possible wanted to tell him about the operation but knew that would be another thing Charlie would be upset about.

"I been talking to GG and Sabrina a lot too," Possible said.

"If you offerin another excuse, I ain't buyin it."

"Not an excuse, just an explanation," Possible shot back. Explanation, huh?"

"What's been goin on wit everythin? How's Maddy and BJ doin?" Possible asked, trying to change topics.

"Man, that's why I be on you bout callin. Of course I be worried bout you, but also I be needin someone that I trust to vent to." This caught Possible off guard. Was this Charles "Charlie"

Givens being vulnerable, admitting to his best friend and right-hand man, that he needed him? This concerned Possible. Even when Possible had volunteered to take the rap for the Russian incident, Charlie hadn't been this vulnerable.

"Bro, you know I'm here for you. What's goin on?" Possible asked.

"You know I pride myself on always bein the rock for the family. I'm always makin sure the fam is good. That was easy cause you were out here wit me. I trust you. You gonna give it to me without cut.... You feel the same way I do—family first, everythin else comes after."

"Bro, you scarin me. What's goin on? Did somebody die? Is BJ aight?"

"Naw, everybody good. Maddy just told me she's pregnant."

"Congrats. You always wanted a sibling for BJ," Possible replied, trying to act surprised.

"Yeah, I know, but now's not a good time."

"What you mean 'not a good time'?"

"I been tryna keep it on the low. I'm fightin my third strike for assault. I figured was nothin to talk bout cause the dude wasn't gonna go to the police—till I got pulled over and went to jail for a warrant for assault wit a deadly weapon."

"What the fuck! How long ago was this, and how did Maddy not find out?"

"Man, this was 'round the time Maddy and Sabrina came to visit. I had Jim bail me out before Maddy could figure it out."

Possible sat shocked, at a loss for words.

"I been meanin to tell you, but I could never find the right time. Jim said we got action of gettin it dropped to a lesser, but the prosecutor might wanna play hardball."

"Who you get into it wit?"

"Man, it's a long story, but basically niggas tried to rob me."

This told Possible that Charlie knew who it was, because Charlie only dealt with people he knew.

"Aight, one step at a time. How far along are you in the court process?"

"Jim still tryna find out the basics, so not that far along; worst case go to trial, best case it gets dropped to a lesser. No way I can avoid prison time; it's gonna come down to how much," Charlie explained.

"You're lookin at this all wrong. Best case is *no* prison time if this guy don't show up for trial."

"That's what I'm waitin on from Jim," Charlie replied, sounding confident.

"Damn, Peety, this a tough spot, but we gonna figure it out… we always do."

"I just dint want you to feel I let you down," Charlie said. Possible understood what Charlie was saying without him having to say it.

"Look, fam, everythin happens for a reason. I understand how you feel right now, but don't beat yourself up over it. Everythin gonna work out the way it supposed to…. I got somethin I been wantin to talk to you bout as well."

"What's that?" Charlie asked.

"So—"

"You have sixty seconds remaining!"

"Call Sabrina and tell her bout this convo we just had."

"You have thirty seconds remaining."

"…and tell her to tell you everythin—the money and all."

"You talking bout the money from the club?" Charlie asked.

Before Possible could respond the call was cut off. Possible was trying to be positive and optimistic for Charlie, but Charlie was right—prison time was inevitable. That thought alone took Possible's breath away; he knew that with a newborn, Maddy would have a nervous breakdown if she lost Charlie to prison.

Possible was so deep in thought that he never even heard the guard yell, "Yard closed."

Seeing everyone lined up on the fence derailed his train of thought. Charlie's looking at prison time just changed everything. It was one thing for Possible to be locked up and still able to help Charlie on the street, but both Charlie and Possible locked up, leaving the women to take care of the fam? This was not to say that they couldn't, but from a financial standpoint, they'd never had to. Possible spoke to no one during his entire walk back to the unit; he thought only of how to prepare for the worst. With the way things were going, it was time to expand the operation. Possible knew it could be done, and he had a head start. Now he would have to build on the foundation he and his crew had already built. Possible replayed their conversation; he'd never seen this side of Charlie, so vulnerable, admitting Possible was needed. This was like Superman having a human moment, and it was enough for Possible to know the situation was worse than Charlie was admitting. With Charlie on his way back to prison, and Maddy about to have a baby, Possible realized that his secret about the operation would be just what Charlie needed, which was not to say it would solve all their problems, but it would make coming back to prison easier to deal with.

Chapter 20

Hang Up and Cuff Up

It'd been three weeks to the day since Charlie had told Possible about the inevitability of a prison sentence, and not a day had passed without Possible talking to Charlie. Just as Possible had predicted, Charlie was proud of him, and let him know it by giving advice on the operation. It was just like the old days, Charlie and Possible making it happen for the fam, only this time it was Possible telling Charlie, "We do this cause we have to, not cause we want to. When our paper right we do what we want to."

Over the past three weeks, Possible had developed tunnel vision. He considered sharing the Charlie situation with his clique, then decided not to, but everyone who knew Possible noticed the change.

"Mr. Jenkins, would you help me unload the property truck?" CO Hunter said. To anyone who was listening it sounded like she was giving Possible the option to help or not, but he knew this was a direct order.

"We bout to have yard in a minute, and I need to use the phone," Possible replied with enough irritation to make Hunter feel less important than his need to make a call.

"I'll make sure you get to use the phone if you miss yard," Hunter replied with the same degree of irritation. Her response made Possible feel guilty for showing his frustration.

"No problem. I got you. When will you need me?" Possible asked, trying to clean it up.

"I need you now," Hunter said, and began to walk in the opposite direction on her way to the property room. Possible followed right behind her.

"My bad for the attitude—"

"Shh!" We're about to load property first," Hunter said in a professional tone. Possible got the hint.

"It's been a very busy week," Hunter announced.

"Busy three weeks for me," Possible replied.

"I'd be lying if I said I hadn't noticed," Hunter whispered as the two entered the property room.

"Yeah, my family been goin through it, and I feel part to blame cause I'm in here."

"You can't blame yourself or allow their problems to become your problems," CO Hunter said, grabbing a box from the shelf to load onto the cart. Her statement irritated Possible, but he didn't blame her. *She don't know what my family means to me.*

"I know you don't understand my family problems are my problems," Possible explained, with more passion than he intended.

"I apologize. I didn't mean to sound insensitive to what your family is going through."

"It's okay," Possible replied, taking a box from her hands and making contact with her fingers in the process. The contact was subtle, but the feeling was sensual, and it created an awkward silence.

"My bad," Possible said breaking the awkward silence.

"What if I was okay with that… and I want more of it?" CO Hunter replied while she loaded the box.

It seemed that Possible didn't reply fast enough.

"There's only one answer I want to hear," Hunter said. "If it's not that, then it's best you don't say anything.

Shocked, Possible froze as he were staring at a winning lottery ticket, trying to make sure the numbers matched. CO Hunter, herself confused, pushed the cart out of the property room without another word. Alone, Possible snapped back to reality; he darted through the door and, regaining his composure, knew exactly how to answer her question. As he turned the corner to catch up with Hunter, he saw the truck driver helping her unload the property. Possible took his time and casually joined them. While the driver and CO Hunter were making small talk, Possible eyed Hunter the entire time, with no care in the world whether the driver noticed.

"Excuse me, sir, it's rude to stare," The trucker announced, making CO Hunter uncomfortable.

"Oh, he's just upset I made him miss big yard," Hunter replied, trying to make light of the situation.

"What if I was okay with that?" Possible replied without breaking eye contact. CO Hunter turned beet red. The two had a moment for the first time since Possible had started helping her. They held eye contact briefly, but to them it felt like an eternity.

"Well, I got more property to drop off. Take care of yourself, Jamie!" the truck driver announced, feeling the chemistry between the other two.

"Take it easy, Mark!" CO Hunter replied, coming back to reality.

"Watch yourself," Mark warned before taking off. The walk to the property room was silent, but the sensual energy was louder than a Seattle Seahawks game. As soon as the two entered the property room, CO Hunter said, "Mr. Jenkins that is totally unacceptable we have to—"

Before she could finish her sentence, Possible had backed her into a corner, his arms wrapped tightly around her waist, his tongue so far down her throat she was forced to breathe through her nose.

"Jenkins!" Possible ignored the plea and began to caress her breasts and buttocks.

"No, Jenkins, wait… wait."

Possible was so caught up in the moment that he forgot where the two of them were.

"Wait, we can't right now, not like this," Hunter said, pushing Possible away.

"How's that answer?" Possible asked in a seductive whisper. Hunter got lost in Possible's gaze, at a loss for words till she'd begun to fix herself.

"First things first: Never ever act like that in front of my coworkers. I'm not trying to lose my job. Thank god Mark is like a brother to me. Secondly don't tell anyone, Washington especially, and last but not least, never make me feel like I don't matter to you," Hunter demanded.

"You do matter to me; my family is just in a tough spot so I got a lot on my mind."

"I understand. I'm here for you. Whatever I can do to help, just let me know. Anytime you need someone to talk to, I want to be that person," Hunter said.

"Now that we established that, I'll be aware of your wants and needs as well, and whatever else you want me to be," Possible said, which made her flash the most beautiful smile Possible had ever seen. As CO Hunter walked out of the property room, she grabbed a handful of Possible's manhood on the way. As he walked out behind her, Possible was in another world, that place where problems and stress don't exist, but as soon as the unit door opened and he entered the dayroom, paradise quickly evaporated and reality set in: Charlie was on his way to prison.

The past few weeks had been bittersweet for Possible. His relationship with CO Hunter had made things a little awkward between Possible and Sabrina. Possible had loved Sabrina since they were in elementary school. Their relationship was complicated—off and on for the past ten years, neither able to remain faithful to the other. Throughout the years, an unspoken code had developed. No matter what was going on in their lives, or who their significant other was, they would always be there for one another, putting nothing ahead of each other. The situation worked for Possible and Sabrina. In fact, it brought them closer and strengthened their bond.

Possible felt it might be different this time around. The idea of another woman taking Sabrina's place made talking to her awkward. Possible had never kept secrets from her, nor she from him. He just didn't know how to explain the situation or what the situation actually was. After all, it'd only been a few weeks since his strong feelings for Hunter had surfaced. Possible felt he owed it to Sabrina to at least try to address the discomfort they both felt. He dialed her number.

"Hello?" I'm glad you called, Possible. I was just emailing you," Sabrina said, anxiety in her voice. "Things been a li'l weird between us—"

"I been feelin the same way," Possible said.

"I know, baby. I know you been feelin it too, and it's not fair."

Possible knew it was difficult, but the way Sabrina sounded made him feel guilty—he knew he should have told her about Hunter. "Aight, baby, I was gonna—"

"No, wait!" Sabrina snapped, cutting him off. Let me finish! I was waitin for the right time to tell you, but I had to wait till I was a hundred percent sure," she said.

Instantly, a knot formed in Possible's throat, making it hard to speak.

"Sure of what?"

A hesitant response made Possible's heart drop into his stomach. Feeling his dismay through the phone made Sabrina burst into tears.

"I love you so much," Sabrina replied trying to stop her overwhelming emotions. Possible sat in silence, bracing himself for the worst. He'd forgotten all about telling Sabrina about Hunter.

"What's good? You can talk to me bout anythin," Possible said nervously.

"I'm pregnant!" Sabrina said, bursting into tears.

"What the fuck you mean, you're pregnant?!"

"I just left the doctor's office. I been sick and missed my period, but I wanted to make sure," Sabrina said.

Possible's head began to spin. He was unaware of Sabrina's sobbing, which was drowned out by a baby's crying and a man's voice that wasn't his shouting at Sabrina.

"Who's the father?" Possible asked, holding his emotions in check.

"Mike," Sabrina answered in a whisper.

"Meezy?" Possible snapped.

Sabrina's lack of an answer said it all. Michel Humphrey, aka Meezy, whom Possible knew all too well. Possible's archenemy, whom he had met in elementary school, the same school where he'd met Sabrina. In fact, it was Meezy who'd introduced Possible to Charlie. Meezy and Possible became best friends. When Possible moved to Washington from Elgin, the two were inseparable until after their graduation, when Meezy had dated Sabrina despite knowing how Possible felt about her. It had been warlike competition ever since. In fact, Possible had started dating Meezy's sister just to get revenge. Sabrina had finally seen that Meezy was more obsessed with Possible than with her, so she chose Possible after learning how he really felt about her. Until now, Possible felt he'd won the battle, but a sense of having lost the war now gave way to jealousy.

"You're not havin his baby!" Of all people, why him?"

"He came to the club one night and apologized for what happened when we were kids, and I had a vulnerable moment. We only messed round once. He was tryna get serious, but I told him I would never love him the way I love you," Sabrina said.

"What about the first part of my question?"

"You have sixty seconds remaining."

Sabrina had always hated the robot voice telling you the call was ending, but right then she couldn't have been happier to hear it.

"I guess that's somethin we're gonna have to talk about," she replied.

"You have thirty seconds remaining!"

"There's nothin to talk bout," Possible snapped.

"You know how I feel bout abortions," Sabrina said softly.

You know how I feel bout Meezy," Possible shot back.

A click told Possible that the call was over—maybe he and Sabrina were over as well. A wave of anger washed over him, and being unable to confront Meezy made it all the more intense. A hint of calm ran through his body at the realization that if he couldn't get to Meezy, Charlie could. The unit clock showed five minutes till dayroom was over. As the phone rang, Possible thought of how, with no time to explain why, he could tell Charlie to whip Meezy's ass. Possible was caught off guard when Maddy answered the phone.

"Hello?" Sobbing, Maddy struggled to speak.

"What's wrong, and where's Charlie?" Possible asked, Maddy was breathing so hard she could barely get the words out.

"On his way to prison!" Maddy replied, bursting into tears.

"What happened?"

The dayroom intercom blared: "Dayroom closed! Lock up! Cell in!"

"I just dropped him off to start his sentence."

"I thought he was goin to trial, and everythin was figured out."

"I don't know," Maddy sobbed. The dayroom horn began to blow, alerting the guards.

"Let's go! Lockup!" a CO began to yell at Possible.

"How much time he get?" Possible asked, ignoring a direct order.

"I don't know!"

Maddy's lack of knowledge began to frustrate Possible.

"Maddy, what the fuck's goin on?" he yelled, loud enough to make two COs approach him. "What the fuck you mean, you don't know? What did he tell you?" Possible demanded, shouting into the phone.

"Hey! Hang up the phone or you're goin to the hole!" one of the CO's yelled. Possible hadn't realize the two guards had been shouting direct orders till it was too late.

"All he said was he needed me to turn him in. He had to take a deal, things dint go how his lawyer thought they would," she said, trying to calm herself.

As Maddy's words began to sink in, Possible turned around to see that everyone had locked down and a group of guards were running through the dayroom toward him. Unaware that the two CO's had called a code, meaning there was an incident requiring the use of force, Possible saw the two COs for the first time, and heard them yelling, "Hang up and cuff up." Tears began to fall from his eyes.

"I love you, Maddy. Everythin gonna be aight, I promise."

Maddy began to cry hysterically, shouting *Why?* so loudly that when Possible dropped the phone to cuff up he could still hear her cries. Possible couldn't' hear anything the guards were saying, only Maddy's coughing, sobs, and her repeated *Why?* She was screaming it now, and Possible wondered how long she could continue. As the guards began to walk Possible away from the phones, Maddy's crying got louder. It wasn't until Possible had made it out of the dayroom that he realized Maddy had hung up the phone long before. Whatever the guards were saying to him, all Possible could hear was Maddy's sobs, coughing, and *Why?*—all the way to the hole.

Chapter 21

The Hustle Continues

"Possible!… Possible!… Possible!" A familiar voice woke him. For the past three days Possible had been dead to the world. It wasn't until a day ago that he finally realized he was in the hole. This time he didn't care if he ever came out; he wasn't even sure he wanted to live anymore. He'd never commit suicide, so he would do the next best thing: lie under the blankets and pretend to be dead.

"Possible! Is that you?" the voice yelled. "Get yo ass up!"

Possible sluggishly made his way to his cell window.

"What's good, my nigga?" Possible followed the familiar voice with his eyes and found Dam'on staring out his cell window.

"What happen?" Dam'on asked.

"I don't know!" Possible yelled back.

"Why you in the program pod?"

"I don't know why!" As the words left Possible's lips, Maddy's despairing voice crept back into his head.

"It's all good, bro. Ay, get your line ready. I'm bout to slide down to you."

It took Possible a moment to understand what Dam'on was talking about.

After giving Possible a few minutes to make a fishing line, Dam'on yelled, "You see me?… Possible!… Possible!"

"Yeah, I see you."

"Pull me in!" Dam'on said.

"Aight, I got you," Possible yelled.

As Possible began to pull, he wondered what Dam'on was sending him. He knew it couldn't be what he thought it might be.

"You get the envelope?" Dam'on asked.

Possible was opening the envelope without answering. Inside was a note and a piece of plastic. The site of the plastic brought him instant joy. Possible began to scan the cell for an outlet. Reality set in and his joy quickly evaporated. Feeling defeated again, he read the note:

What's good, li'l bro? I hope all is well. I been hearing a lot of good things about you out there. We got a lot to talk about, but you're in long-term hole, so we'll be here. Here's a li'l something to snap you back.

Possible began to unwrap the plastic and saw tiny pieces of a glass-like substance. Possible had a flashback to the Russian incident and realized he was holding meth. Possible reread the note and saw he'd forgotten to read the postscript.

"PS: Crush it and snort it like powder, and let's get this money. This shit doesn't stop."

Possible was hesitant. He began to think about Sabrina and Meezy, Charlie and Maddy, what all this meant for the fam. Feeling overwhelmed, he began to crush the substance aggressively, scraped the powder into a line, and snorted through the note Dam'on had sent. A very intense burn followed by a head rush such as he'd never experienced. Five minutes later Possible felt a euphoria that couldn't be put into words. It was like an ecstasy pill times ten. Possible's knees began to get weak. He lay on his back and stared at the ceiling. All his problems began to float away, everything that had ever stressed him or felt problematic began to turn into solutions. As the negatives transformed into positives, the ceiling evaporated. Parts of Possible's brain were operating on another plane, parts that he'd had no clue existed. He was staring into the universe, seeing moons, stars, and galaxies. Whatever Possible questioned, wondered, or felt uncertain about, the answers flashed across the universe. Not understanding what he was experiencing, he decided not to fight it but to embrace it, and he relaxed, crossing his hands behind his head. Charlie and Maddy, Meezy and Sabrina. Meezy quickly evaporated, replaced by an image of Sabrina and Possible. His future flashed before him, and a huge smile appeared on his face. He knew exactly what to do and how to do it!

Glossary

Bid: Refers to confinement or the length of a prison sentence.

Breezeway: Long, wide sidewalks that inmates use to travel from one destination to another, interspersed with locking gates for security.

Car: Used to describe different groups/cliques/gangs; typically, each has a "driver" (leader) who holds the keys.

Chow Hall: A space about the size of a school cafeteria, where meals are served to inmates.

Closed custody: The most restricted condition, designated for inmates who are removed from the general population for disciplinary or administrative reasons. It allows for less movement, is segregated, and is more violent.

Count: Scheduled period of time when there is no movement and guards count the inmates for security purposes.

Joog: The sale of drugs; a person buying drugs; charity/helping someone out.

Lighter: Made using three pieces of pencil lead; two go directly into an electrical outlet, while the third is used to strike the ends of the two that protrude from the outlet, thus creating a spark. A small piece of cotton is used to catch the spark and create a flame.

Mainline: Breakfast, lunch, dinner, where pod/units are called to chow hall. Biggest movement on prison compound. Can also be a reference to general population.

Pod/Unit: Living quarters where the incarcerated are housed.

Security check: Cell inspection, which consists of entering the cell, banging on walls to check for holes, flushing toilets, turning lights off and on, and removing any found contraband.

Tier: The walkway around and between cells in the unit.

Tier Check: Every hour or so, a guard will walk the tier and look in on each cell as a security and wellness precaution.

Tray Up: Throw away uneaten food, return tray, and leave the chow hall.

Yard: Recreation time outdoors.

King Pen: The Rise of a Penitentiary King

After celebrating his twenty-fourth birthday, Charles (Charlie) Givens, along with childhood best friend, Pierre "Possible" Jenkins, find themselves in a drug deal gone terribly wrong. What was supposed to be a life-changing opportunity quickly became a homicidal nightmare. A last-minute decision would be made that would forever alter the lives of these two men. One was inspired by love and family, while the other aspired to be king!